T0146838

Facade

Facade

A collection of stories celebrating the
strength of the Nigerian Woman

EBIYE LAVONNE GARMEL-URUMEDJI

FACADE
A collection of stories celebrating the strength of the Nigerian Woman

iUniverse books may be ordered through booksellers or by contacting:

iUniverse
1663 Liberty Drive
Bloomington, IN 47403
www.iuniverse.com
1-800-Authors (1-800-288-4677)

ISBN: 978-1-5320-0153-6 (sc)
ISBN: 978-1-5320-0152-9 (e)

Library of Congress Control Number: 2016911041

Print information available on the last page.

iUniverse rev. date: 07/21/2016

DEDICATION

To my mother.... Mrs. Ruth Adjoa Botu
For the countless times you stood by me...
For my burdens, you helped make lighter....
For your wonderful genes and beautiful spirit I inherited.
My Mother... the perfect example of a true Nigerian woman.

To my daughter... Cherelle Efe Ebiteme,
The future Nigerian woman,
God will continually grant me wisdom to inspire you positively,
And teach you how to differentiate facts from wishes,
As I have come to learn that 'realistic' thinking
Produces a wonderfully fulfilled life.
God help me.

To all Nigerian women...
Especially those from the Southern part of Nigeria.
They are plagued with so many limitations;
both ancestral and physical-yet stood strong.

ACKNOWLEDGEMENT

I, first and foremost want to thank God Almighty
For the gift instilled in me,
And to my right hand pal; the Holy Spirit for direction….

Second in line is my Treasure, my hubby- Garmel Urumedji.
Thank you my love, for being a unique breed of Naija husband.
Your love for me is without a doubt my greatest blessing
I would be lost without you….
Thanks for Loving Me Babes…..I Love You!

I doff my hat for my Parents –Elder & Mrs. James Botu…
Your unshakable faith in me and
Your dedication to my childhood years made me who I am today.
The foundation you laid is just too solid,
NOTHING has been able to shake it. I love you 'Pale and Male'

Much Love to my lovely sister -Botu Ebiteme Joy
for believing in me and never doubting for a second, my potentials.

Heavens appreciation to my Pastor….Pst Korede Komaiya (Kay Kay)
President and founder of The Master's Place International Church.
For years I have been your faithful sheep,
Thanks for been the best life coach.
I celebrate you Sir!!

Lots of kisses to my first fruit-my son Derek,
for playing with his siblings while I focus and write.

INTRODUCTION

In 2 days, my newborn baby daughter will be three (3) weeks old… my daughter named so carefully almost two weeks ago as follows:

Cherelle	-	the beloved one
Efetobore	-	I have received wealth
Ebiteme	-	good spirit
Oritsetsemaye		God has done well for me
Tamaradenyefah		Nothing supersedes God

We carefully and prayerfully chose these names to have a positive impact on her life.

I, in particular plan to leave no stone unturned in training and molding her into a "woman after God's own heart" This is my solemn priority and I will follow it to the latter.

As I gaze into her beautiful face… my heart aches for the world in which she has been born into. Not really the world at large but the part of the world she may grow up in; the West African part of the African continent.

For the past twenty-three months I have carried a burden in my heart. Far away in Vorna Valley, Midrand-Johannesburg South Africa I started writing this book.

I was exposed to marriage in another culture. I took note of the way women were treated and respected and the confidence with which they carry themselves. I was awed. But one funny phenomenon I encountered was; West African marriages are West African marriages. It doesn't matter that they are not resident in Nigeria; so long both parties are West-Africans-especially Nigerians the women suffer the same plague…

Today I sit and ponder… how can our lives as women be made better? What principles needed to be changed? How will these changes come about? Who will enforce it? Who will fight for it? Who will speak up?

As I write, my head is filled with pictures of sad, depressed, frustrated, abused women. my ears hear their cry… my heart weeps with them and understand the depth of their heartache… and I die all over again…

Is this the plight my newborn daughter would be initiated into? Is this the culture and tradition that will be shoved down her throat? Eisshhh!!!

Following are stories of different women, who struggled through unique challenges and faced them as African Women. It is paramount that you realize that people differ and so are their challenges. Their stories are straight from the heart and are not pretentious. They tell their stories the way they feel it, in their unique ways.

STORY 1

Timi's story

The clock on the sitting room wall says "four pm" ... There's a sharp jab of pain that just ran through my heart ... almost too fast I could hardly acknowledge it... but I knew it happened and I know for the next couple of hours, I will be feeling more of that.

Hmmm...... it's now six fifty-five pm and I can't help but go out to the window facing the street watching and waiting.... Waiting.... yes.... waiting!

The kids are through with homework, have had their bath and have had dinner ... safely tucked in their room watching a kiddie's channel, waiting for lights out.

Do they feel the tension? Do they feel this agonizing pain? This fear filled anxiety? This fear that runs through my being...I hope not... I sincerely hope not... No human deserves to feel this way... No one!

"Honk! Honk!! Honk!" My heart jumped to my mouth... Adrenalin all over the place... I couldn't feel my face, my hands and my feet!

I glanced at the clock once more, it says nineteen forty-five pm... I rushed to the window, shaking terribly... I could hear my heart pounding... it's so loud I am sure the kids can hear it...

Peeping through the window.... "Hmmmm" sign of relief... it's not my gate... I walked back to the sitting room... sat down and tried desperately hard to concentrate on the movie on screen but how can I? How? Just how?

Even at rest now, my heart beats very fast. I don't need a doctor to tell me I have developed high blood pressure... "Doctor..." a bitter smile danced on my lips "a doctor!" I can't even afford to pay to see a doctor.

My heart leaped and began beating faster... the thought of the doctor reminded me of the sorry state my health was in...

Today is the twenty sixth day of my menstrual period... Hot tears flows down my cheeks... day twenty six!!! More tears, bitter tears...

How could this be? How long will this menstrual period last? The last one was for forty one days... *sob*sob*sob*... (I don't even want to go there).

I already feel so sore down there... My whole private aches ... I can't afford sanitary pads and the small towels I cut into small sizes are all faded out... am so scared to continue using them... The tissue paper I use (a cheap one of course) makes life terrible for me.

I have to wear tight shorts to help protect it from falling off to avoid any embarrassment. It then occurred to me that I need to go change it...I stood up and slowly headed to the bathroom.

"Day Twenty six!!! Tomorrow Day twenty seven!!! Tears still rolling down my cheek... God please have mercy!! Please have mercy!! This is too much...

Sitting in the loo has always been a great comfort for me. Right from childhood, I feel relaxed when I am sitting in "my toilet"

Sitting down here brought some moments of peace...I felt a little calm and pondered the root cause of this elongated menstrual period.

Sometimes I go seven to nine weeks without getting my period and not because I am pregnant. And when it does come, it lasts for as long as it wishes... I have heard of the stupendous bills been charged by gynecologist for diagnostic test and subsequent treatments, I can't even wrap my mind around the figures... it's completely out of my reach.

'Deborah' The name of a friend, who is also seeking the fruit of the womb, had approached me earlier in the year to come with her to a "mama" as they are fondly called. "Mama's" are tradomedical/midwives that treat with live plants and locally sourced herbs... They also offer massages and they help to reposition the uterus of women who have prolapsed uterus...

I have never heard of this predicament I find myself... A menstrual period that is supposed to last three to seven days at most has now turned into a nightmare. The shortest period I have had in the past year is sixteen days... Even that to some women I know will be too much to bear. I have been through a lot.

My mind went to the native drugs they give that is made with alcoholic drinks...I don't take alcohol and I wonder how my body will cope with the drug. I was told the minimum I will be charged is two thousand naira (thirteen dollars) and it can go as high as fifty thousand naira (three hundred dollars) ... Nothing comes cheap these days...

"Ring! Ring!! Ring!!!" The sound of my phone ringing shook me out of my deep thoughts...

Caller ID shows it's "Hubby"... The sharp pain jabbed at my heart again ...

"Let this be good ... oh Lord!!" I prayed silently as I answered.

I could barely hear what he was saying "Oh my God! He is tipsy already? This can't be good"...

"Bye baby..." He hung up... Tears streamed down my face. Heart pounding as it usual does. He's going to be home late. I checked my phone... its eleven-thirty pm. How late can late be! No precise hour... and He is already tipsy.

God help me... And I have to be up, wide awake waiting to serve him dinner or breakfast determining when he gets home.

"Let me check on the kids", I thought to myself, rising to leave the toilet. They were both sound asleep... I sat beside the bed and watched them sleep.

My Treasures, My Pride, My World. Whenever I look at them, my heart gladdens, and I don't feel like a failure. How did I get so lucky?

How did God know just the perfect antidote to soothe my aching heart? That's why He is God! My twins; My Everything.

Tears flowing down my face I remembered the day I had them, ten hours of excruciating pain. It was a rainy day in May and I was in the second floor of the hospital, watching the tall trees dance in rhythm to the wind and the rain. It was cold, really cold but it had no effect on the lightening and earthquake-like pains shooting all around my pelvic, hip and anus... I remember singing out all the names of Jehovah... Elohim, Shammah, Shalom and the rest... and for some funny reason... I thought long and hard about Adam and Eve... I meditated for long on what really transpired at the Garden of Eden.

I wondered deeply. And in my pain, tried to replay the events that happened at the Garden of Eden, in different ways. I was wishing very hard that Eve could have just played dumb. And the love-stricken Adam, couldn't he have been a man? Heck! Men these days are so bully-head. I know; I married one. Why was Adam so weak? And the serpent... I remembered hissing...Good riddance...

Then my mind went to God... and all the lovely things He said about us, His children... The sweet and caring promises. Now that am in labor and has been under pains for nine hours plus straight, I couldn't wrap my mind around the fact that God really did love me... if he did, why would he allow me go through this pain... this bone wrecking, vein squeezing, excruciating pain... I remember screaming out to the amazement of my mum, my sister-in-law and my hubby who were there with me...

"Eve... it can never be well with you!! Couldn't you just be dumb? Couldn't you have just walked away from that slimy, ugly looking creature called the serpent... because of your foolishness... see what I am going through... Grrrrrrrhrrhh!!"

And "My heavenly father? You that is greater than the greatest, bigger than the biggest, mightier than the mightiest, don't you think this punishment is a little too much? I can feel my babies fighting hard to clear the path... Are they guilty too???... Ohhhhh!!! Gooodddd! And what do the men get? Just to feed us?-to till the ground, as you put it! Are women not bread winners these days? Women are playing the role of breadwinners all around the world and doing a very great job at it. Can't we have substitutes to labor pains like men do?

And I swear I heard a still small voice saying....

"Epidural and Caesarean section are substitutes dear"....

"Grrrhhh....... But they are also painful!!" I replied whining. My mum and hubby walked closer to me trying to see if I am going mad...

From then everything was a blur... I remember getting the urge to push... and began pushing out of my own eve-like wisdom...

I heard the doctor screaming out, "she's ready... take her to the delivery room..."

I was shocked...anger rising fast from deep within me. I remember screaming at the doctor,

"Take me where? Take me where? What happened to this bed I am lying on?"

"This is the first stage room, for the laboring stage" He answered...

"Oh! Oh! Wow!!! So you knew all along that this is not where I am going to deliver and you kept me here.*long hissing* ...okay watch me!!!" and I started pushing...

"Madam please" the doctor pleaded....

"Timi please, don't push, you will harm your babies" my mum chipped in.

She could have been talking to a rock for all I cared. "One, two and three..." I kept on counting, getting ready to push again...

My mind jumped and went to Mary the Virgin Mother of Jesus... and my mind began joggling the facts... Virgin birth?????... No breakage in birth canal???... Is it a myth??? Then I scolded myself...

"Tiiiimmiii!" "Oh Tiiiimmmi!!"....

"Hush! Hush!!... That's the Son of God you are talking about..." I whispered to myself... "The God who separated the land from the sea... The day from night... with whose powers Moses divided the Red sea... What then is a tiny birth canal, mushied up with folded tissues and a small patch work closing the entrance called hymen?...

All of a sudden...I was Mary, in the manger alone... Joseph outside... Outside??? Jeez...why didn't he help? He just stood out

there? Men! *Rolling my eyes*... my pain became one with Mary's ....
And I imagined that I was the one with the closed birth canal....

"Oh! Oh!! Mary!! Mary!! Maarrryyyy!!! Poor you!!! Is this what
you went through? Oh boy!! Whatever the catholics call you... you
sure do deserve it"

I knew everyone with me then would have concluded that I was
going mad. And they were not far from the truth.... I was going
insane with pains... I remembered an article I read where it said that
the highest level of pain the human body can stand is forty six (46)
del-whatever the hell del stands for... and this forty six (46) del is
equivalent to all the bones in the human body being crushed at the
same time... that's the same amount of pains forty six del represents...
but at the time of child birth, the pain a woman experiences is fifty
seven del. Can you beat that...?

My heart began to pound.... Is the fifty seven del what I have
been experiencing all day or am I yet to experience it... by now I was
on the delivery table... baby one.... Rearing to come out....

"Blood of Jesus!! Give me strength... fifty-seven del of pain...
fifty-seven del of pain... isn't this too much? All this as a result of
listening to a damned serpent!"

I remembered something about the after birth... the delivery of
the placenta ... I had two ... I thought about episiotomy.... Will the
doctor have to tear me? If not, will the babies tear me?

"Come on Timi! Too much information is only doing you harm
at this moment." Always reading, always wanting to know more...
At this point been as dumb as possible would do me a great deal of
Good... I always thought to be forewarned is to be forearmed... I
felt knowing what lies ahead would help me understand things much
better, giving me a clear perspective... at this moment, right now ...
I didn't think so...

"Honk! ... Honk!!.... Honk!!!"....

"I jumped from my reverie". I ran to the sitting room, checked the
time, twenty five past one (one twenty-five am) ... I ran as fast and as
quietly as I could to the door, and sped right down through the stairs
(we live in an apartment building and shared staircases) to check the

stair door… quietly as possible, trying not to alert the neighbors… also silently thanking God that he didn't get to the door before me, if not the whole neighborhood would be awake… and there was light… if PHCN(in charge of electricity distribution in Nigeria) has strucked, at least generators and plants would be on… I have been always lucky that the days that were really bad, where shouting and all that follows took place… Light was always out… so the loud noisy generators had been the saving grace for me for the past eight years of emotional, verbal and physical abuse that has been dished out to me as regularly as three times a week on the average…

Still standing by the stair door, I watched as a figure staggered forward… swaying from side to side… No shirt on… only sparkling white singlet… shirt on one shoulder… swaying, swaying, swaying holding whatever was close to him for support… tears filled my eyes… as I watched my husband, the father of my children, the one I had high hopes about and had hoped God would use as an instrument to bring out the wonderful gifts in me… all expectations now replaced with gross disappointment…

I caught him just as he was about to fall down… and helped support him as he climbed the stairs… In my heart I was praying he goes to bed on time… God help me!! God help me!!!... Please … I have a busy day tomorrow…

He fell on the bed like a log of wood… the smell of alcohol filled the room. The way a cheap perfume would hold a room ransom with their pungent smell…

"My food! Let me have my food now… or am I going to sleep on an empty stomach"? He screamed.

I was shaking, confused as to whether to take off his shoes first or run to the kitchen… at such times… any mistake could lead to hot slaps… those types that makes you forget momentarily where you are and you can still hear the tingle for some brief seconds after you have been dealt…

I decided to dash to the kitchen…I quickly microwaved the fresh fish banga soup, with fresh shrimps, periwinkle and oyster. Did the same for the pounded yam… arranged the tray and practically ran back to the room... praying he hasn't fallen asleep-that will spell trouble...I don't need to go into thoughts of nights, when he slept on empty stomach and woke me up in wee hours of the morning with demeaning words... lets not ply that route tonight....

Door opened, I took a quick peak...accessing the situation stealthily, like a soldier at the enemy's camp...he isn't snoring yet (good sign). I woke him up, and he began eating, while I stood watching.

One of these days I am going to video him and show him in the morning...

"Perish that thought... Timi!"...

"You can't guess the outcome of that day"...

"Good advice" I thought to myself.

Watching him eat is heartbreaking. Let me try and create a picture. He takes a lump of pounded yam... sometimes both eyes closed, at a time only one eye open... He raises his hand up and searches for his mouth... like a baby seeking the nipple to his mother's breast... He finds it... swallows and if it's a piece of meat, he lies down back on the bed and chews... then he sits up again swaying and again balances himself...he reaches forth and takes another lump, sways back and forth... trying to balance himself once again.... Searches hard for his mouth... finds it... at this time, he is already lying on his side... He swallows ... sits up again, searches for the glass of water... experience has taught me to remove the water from the tray, because he normally hits it. And series of times when it fell to the floor... venomous words flying out of his mouth as I quickly handed him the glass of water... so I had learnt to always be on standby... he always drinks and lets go of the glass, as if gravity placed it in his hand... I quickly grabbed it.

He is done. I carried the tray back to the kitchen with the mind to race back and take off his cloths. Stacking the plate in the sink, I noticed, he cleaned up!! He ate every morsel... to think that for the past six (6) years I could count the number of times that he had given me money for food, or for school fees ... Not a thought for tonight.

Walking back to the room slowly from exhaustion and lack of sleep, I got the shock of my life. Standing there in the hallway, holding on to the hallway curtain for support was my husband.

Blood drained from my face... my mind went straight to my neighbors... God no generator is on... My secret will be out today...

"Where is my food?" he screamed...

"Where is my food? I came home and you refused to give me food... is this your plan? To kill me with hunger? You want to be the man of the house? To control me? You bad luck woman... I have had nothing but bad luck since the day I met you... He who finds a wife finds a good thing rubbish...not in my case. Witch! Witch!!... Witch!!! ... My mother told me not to marry you... go into the kitchen and get me my food Now!! Nooowww!!!!!!!" He screamed.

God!!!.... Fear paralyzed me...How do I begin to explain that he just downed a plate of pounded yam and fresh fish banga soup? How??....

God give me wisdom ... Solomon's kind... right now or else ... I don't want to imagine what will follow...

I knelt down fast... my heart pounded so loud, I could hear it skip one or two beats... my mind flew to the neighbors yet again...then, my twins... sleeping in the other room...

Please "my love" ... I smiled... In this situation, any slight frown or sad emotion I show will result to questions like "Am I suffering you?" "Why are you acting like the world is ending?" "Why do you act like I am a beast?"... Slaps and manhandling would follow easily.

So I smiled as lovingly as my fear would permit me to ...

"Baby, you just finished eating fresh fish banga soup and pounded yam"

"I am just returning from the kitchen where I went to drop the plates."

He staggered past me to the kitchen... I was still on my knees... both hands clasped together like am in prayer... praying actually, but trying desperately not to look like I am praying... if I am caught praying that would be disastrous...

He returned .... Looked hard at me ... bullet shooting from his eyes ... I kept my face expressionless... and watched him ... still kneeling down...

"Get into the room now ..." He said and walked past me staggering .... "Sex!!" my heart skipped again ... "not tonight please..."

We got to the room; he slumped on the bed still wearing pants and shoes... I helped him out of it... slowly... I checked the clock on the bedroom wall... two thirty eight (2:38am) ... all his item of clothing gone... I noticed he was getting weak...

"I need to go wash up.... Am still bleeding"

He hisses... "Hurry and come back now"...

I walked to the bathroom... and began to wash up slowly... this is officially day twenty seven of my period...

"God... wake me up from this nightmare..."

I couldn't even cry anymore... my heart just kept pounding fast... I knew I was now a high blood pressure patient...

I walked back to the room... He was on the floor rolling from one end to the other... I stood by the door... watching. He rolled to the edge of the wardrobe and began snoring....

"Thank you... Jesus!"

I sneaked back to the bathroom, to pad up my leaking anatomy; 'The woman with the issue of blood'... I finished and sat down for a while for him to sleep deep...

The state he is now... I won't be able to sleep a wink all night... because he has chronic asthma and I need to be on standby... in case he needed to use his ventolin inhaler. I also need to be on standby to position his neck so that there won't be any obstruction to his nasal passage...

After some few minutes, I went back in... I sat on the bed and watched him roll to the other end of the room.... Making terrible sounds... I watched quietly... questions after questions racing through my mind... I thought of women, who are lying in the arms of their husbands... sleeping calmly, after been made sweet love to.

Their needs lovingly taken care of... I have an unfinished job that has to be completed before twelve pm later today. I will need to make breakfast for three and prepare food for the twins to take to school then take the twins to school… We have no vehicle, so I have to walk quiet a distance to get a taxi for them…

And now almost three (3am) I am still up, wide awake… I heard a sound… I looked… it was beloved hubby passing out urine on his body, on the floor right on top of the rug…. I watched the urine spread through his boxers and unto the rug…feeling disgusted and wondering how I will ever able to regain my respect for this man again.

I checked the time again… he will pee like twice again because it's almost dawn…

I rested my head on the pillow… and watched. I remembered how I graduated early with honor's…my head filled with big dreams.

How I was the best corper in my NYSC camp… my decision to pursue my master's degree and all… that was ten year ago… Here I am, at thirty four… with nothing to show… Just a small bedspread business and some pastries I do once in a while.

It's been eight years since I got married…I think about my sister in the US… The other in London… all doing great… I thought about my parents…

My heart aching… my sisters keep telling me how they meet my old classmates who constantly ask if I am currently doing my doctorate… because of the way I was focused and intelligent.

Now my dreams have faded away before my very eyes… if only I asked the right questions. If only I wasn't naïve…"Till death do us part indeed" God am done for…

"No one goes to marriage in our family and returns". I remembered my aunt telling me on my wedding day… "You must endure…no matter what happens you must endure and cover your husband. Don't allow people to see the truth about your home. Don't tell me. Don't tell your mother. Just bear. All men are the same"

I smiled… This is a typical day in my life… I guide my secret very well…. No one knows my pain, not even my sisters… They see me unkempt but they can't ask… they see the passion in life, gone from my eyes, but they are helpless… I have been threatened with death if I leave so many times… I don't even think about it anymore…

I remembered an obituary I saw on a wall, as I went to get my kids from school... she was thirty four (34) married with two kids.... Died of sudden death...

"Hmmmm..."

There's no escape from this life... three months fasting, seventy days fasting, consistent three weeks fasting has yielded no result.... God has turned his back on me...

My mind went back to that poster of the dead woman...

"One day, that would be me..."

.....Timi

STORY 2

Chikas Story

It's been four months since chief my hubby of nine years has been out of this country...

He married me a circumcised virgin at the tender age of seventeen and half going on eighteen... I was practically sold to him, because I didn't really have a choice in the matter. My father was dead and my secondary education was all that was promised me by my poor mother. I had six elder brothers and was the last and only girl in a family of seven.

My elder brothers all had their secondary education and the first three managed to scale through the university before my father died.

Circumstances and destiny brought me before chief. I was to be a bridesmaid at the wedding of a close friend. We were summoned to the bride's father's compound to try on our bridal clothes and see if any alterations will be needed.

I always love to visit my friend's family compound. It's so beautiful and worlds apart from where I grew up. The compound was on a very large piece of land and has so many trees-fruit tress lined the whole fence. Different smell of fruits danced around your nostrils as you stepped into the compound. My favorite is the guava tree. The smell of guava is one of my favorite smell. And the trees are always fruitful all year round. With very delicious fruits always ripe and ready to eat. The soft well-manicured carpet grass below also has a wonderful feel to it. I never hesitate to take of my sandals when I am visiting and always day dream of having a picnic there. I also love the many flowers that are beautifully planted all around the house. The house is a twenty-two (22) room mansion that accommodates their large polygamous family. It's a huge family consisting of sixteen children, five wives and an ailing father. There's always fights and laughter going on around there. Whenever there is a party, the whole place is usually filled to the brim with different activities taking place and it's always loads of fun. So we all look forward to this wedding with great excitement.

While we were having light refreshments of our Nigerian version of small chops-consisting of the famous Nigerian puff-puff (doughnut rounds),samosas, spring rolls, chin chin and peanuts with a glass of juice, we chatted away happily... we were still having fun teasing each other when chief and a host of others arrived...

They entered the compound driving in a convoy of very expensive looking cars. One need not doubt that a very rich personality has arrived. They stepped out of their cars like royalty and walked majestically towards the entrance of the mansion, obviously to pay homage to my friend's father. Their expensive perfume filled the air and made the whole place transformed. When I closed my eyes to take in the beautiful scents dancing on my nostrils, I was catapulted to another time and place. I was no longer the in the village anymore... could that be Miami beach I found myself or was it one of those nice beaches along the coasts of California?

All my friends ogled and looked at them eagerly, fighting and trying desperately to be noticed. We were all beautiful and being young was to our advantage.

Did I mention that I was a beauty to behold? Of course I didn't. Anyways, not one to blow my own trumpet-I am strikingly beautiful in every sense of the word.

My mum made good sure of that. I inherited my fathers light skinned nature and my mum's very long black hair. I am slim, very voluptuously proportioned and very tall at six feet two; pretty tall for my age and has firm pointed breast. I always flaunted it… I wore no bras. And my long straight legs seem to go on forever… my bum was perfectly shaped and fitted for my body. My curves were in all the right places. My friends always tease me that I look like one of those South American soap opera stars; like a top model and I whole heartedly see reason with them. God was very kind to me indeed!

While the other bridesmaid's paraded themselves, going up and about creating a mini show with the way they were going up and about all striving to be seen. I sat still and didn't move an inch.

Why or what rather is the use of parading myself when all six very huge brothers of mine are all back in the village. If I as much as respond to a greeting from the opposite sex, I am sure to be in hot soup. Plus my mum's vigorous daily sermon of kiss and get pregnant vividly plays on without my consent in my head.

But as destiny will have it, chief, not a chief then spotted me and asked whose daughter I was. He was told about our impeccable family history and values and that sealed it.

He came to my house with his family and made known his heart desire. He was sturdily built, evidence that he doesn't joke with his meals. He is handsome and not at all educated but learnt his trade from the tender age of eight. He has and runs a business in Kano (northern Nigeria). He was a very successful businessman as we were told.

So deals were made, promises were kept… like the fact that he flew my three eldest brothers simultaneously oversees for their masters degrees. And the other three were made comfortable in their different higher institutions of their choice.

A large supermarket was been built for my mother at the entrance of the village market, which was completed and stocked soon after my traditional marriage rights were concluded…

Immediately after our white wedding, I was flown to London to visit chief's siblings and to get updated and upgraded. I was smart, so I learnt fast… I was promised a university education after my first child because I got pregnant on our wedding night… a night I swear never to take my mind back to. It was a bitter, bitter experience.

If that was all sex was about, then I better abstain. After spending two months with chief soon after we got married was the UK trip. I was in London till I had my baby; A son. And chief only visited me once while I was pregnant. I was with his sisters all through, while he traveled the whole of Asia hustling to build his empire. He is a very dedicated and hard worker.

He was with us for the naming and dedication of our beautiful son, who was three months old when we took him to church. I was almost nineteen and already picking out schools in England when I started having morning sickness. Home pregnancy test came out positive. My mum was invited to come stay with me, when I was due. I gave birth to twin boys, almost turning twenty.

In twenty two months of marriage, I had three boys and my hubby worshiped me. He is the only son of his parents, so giving him boys was an answer to his prayers.

Five months later I was pregnant again and had to return to Nigeria because my mum refused to stay in England any longer. I returned to England when I was due to give birth and I had another baby boy.

My university education was soon forgotten because at exactly 3 years of marriage I had four kids. Four boys – shoulder to shoulder.

Did I mention that I only get to see my hubby once in three to four months? But I was provided for-like generously provided for. We lacked nothing. I traveled extensively when the kids are on school vacation and we had fun. I had a big mansion in a high brow area to myself and my kids with exotic cars.

Family planning assisted so much in giving me a breathing space but chief won't hear of it. I was young and to him I had enough time to breed and he has gotten the money. He longed so much to have a girl child. I always wonder at the ways of humans. Having four boys should make anyone happy I had thought, until Chief pestered me non-stop for a female child. Hmmm!

So last year I had my last and seventh child... making six boys and one girl. Just like my mum had.

Am turning twenty six and I look as hot as any sexy model can be, it's natural. My mum is still a size twelve at age fifty six. I don't work; I have never worked outside the house or own a business. I don't have lots of friends except for church and other parents at my son's school. And of course the wives of chief's friends who only come in when chief is around.

In a whole year, I get to see my husband for an average of six weeks a year may be less. And to be sincere, I am glad.

We have nothing in common. He is now so big and pot bellied. He never has time for me and I don't worry much. I bought some lubricant that I apply on the rare occasions he remembers to perform his conjugal duties. The lubricant makes my life easy because from start to finish I have no idea about what is going on.

Now back to today. The kids are in bed and am off to night vigil. My mum says she doesn't understand what I am going to pray about in her opinion, my hubby is super rich and the future of the kids are well secured. My brothers are all married and have children. Her business is going well and she too is aging gracefully. My in-laws are all in great shape-so what am I going to pray for exactly? She queried. I laughed and told her that spirituality is a personal race.

Now, I have been faithfully attending night vigils, primarily to build my spirituality. However, two months ago, I ran into a guy I had a crush on while in secondary school. We exchanged pins and started chatting on BBM.

We talked every day, for hours nonstop and we have developed a bond over these past eight weeks. He is married to a career lady who is on cross-posting to another country and they are still childless.

We happen to share loads of mutual interests and one evening the conversation diverted to my sex life. He was like, how do I cope with these long trips chief makes. My nonchalant response saying I don't mind, and that it's not that big a deal, lead to a very lengthy conversation that went on for days. He wondered why I was not interested in sex. I told him I hated it point blank. He told me he had a confession to make and went on to tell me how I make him horny and he goes to sleep with me on his mind. He began sweet talking me with talks about how he longs to kiss me and all. For some time now something sweet has started happening to me; I get excited just thinking about him. I shiver whenever I hear him speak. Is it possible that sex could be nice? Just like I see in the movies?

There's only one way to find out. I'm heading there now and I can't help but notice this tingly feelings running all through my body. What's this?

Let's get one thing straight. I am NEVER leaving chief. Who will care for my battalions? My dear friend said he is not leaving his wife too, so it's a mutual agreement. A one night stand, if I am to define it. I am excited.

Three am following morning.......

I got to the hotel; he was waiting for me in the room. A tastily furnished and sexily decorated room, with sweet smelling candles burning. A table set for two with deliciously looking buffet of food by the side of the table, also were very good wines. I have NEVER been treated to such in my whole life. I felt extra special. Slow music-my favorite kind, filled the air. I could feel the hairs on my body standing. This feeling was strange and new and boy! I Lovvveeed it. We laughed (deep throated laughter) like teenagers. We chatted (I never get to chat with Chief) and he gave me some erotic lecture and asked what I liked but I had no idea.

Hmmmmmm....

Ernest undressed me slowly, I was tensed. He asked me to relax and told me how I looked so, so sexy and pretty and how lucky he was to be holding me in his arms. He began kissing me from my toes slowly up to my thighs, he caressed my private gently and came up to my belly button. He kissed me all the way up to my breast and there he spent some time.

I never knew such pleasure can come out of having a mouth on my nipple. To think these breasts had fed seven babies, wow!

All Chief does is fondle them hard like he wants to burst them and then he proceeds to just turning me to my side, looks for entry point, slams in, do it hard and rolls over. Till next time. I am so grateful to whoever came up with the idea of intimate lubricant.

Back to this sweet moment unfolding before moi…

From one nipple to another; slowly sucking, licking, squeezing while his hands ran through my hair, all over my body. I was shaking, but he wasn't done yet. He kissed me down to my navel and spread my legs. I was tensed and he asked me to relax, reminding me of how beautiful I was beautiful beyond words can say. He praised me and said beautiful words to me.

Then I remembered! And I turned stiff. I tried to explain about my missing clitoris. He told me not to worry, that I was even lucky that a little grew back out. Then he told me to help him locate my G-spot.

"G what?"

Where does this dude think I get the time to start experimenting about such stuff? Raising seven kids is not easy. Its very time consuming. Ask those who have just two then multiply their pressure by two.five (2.5)!

When he got a cold response from me, he ignored my silence and went right ahead and continued where he stopped. He licked and licked, fondled and sucked (at my veejayjay, that's where he is at now, chewing on me as if his life depended on it) I thanked God silently that I remembered to shave and use my delicious scenting intimate wash. I didn't feel much at first. He went on to ask me to relax, close my eyes and imagine my greatest fantasy. I told him I had none. He laughed and told me I was almost a lost cause! I agreed-giggling!

He asked me if I would like to make love on the beach, I giggled some more and answered a very shy yesssss!!!

I was asked to close my eyes and imagine that all that he is doing now, he is doing to me at the beach while we are on a blanket. Having no care if anyone is watching as the cool evening sea breeze caresses our body. As he spoke, I was there already and he went back to licking my clitoris-what's left of it. After like forever, I felt a finger going into my veejayjay; believe it or not, I was wet. He slowly inserted his finger, going in slowly and out so slowly with his mouth still doing his magic.

I began to shiver. He began licking all the way up, sucking my breast while his fingers continued doing their magic down there. His kiss was out of this world (to think I hated kissing prior to this time) before long I was soaked and actually didn't believe that the low deep throated moaning I was hearing was actually mine.

He put on a beautifully colored condom, it was Magenta-my favorite color! I spied his manhood-it was HUGE! The second one I had seen in all of my life. I tried not to compare to Chiefs'. He told me to relax, as he had done all night. He applied some Lubricant to the condom just in case, I guess and held me up lightly and kissed slowly, spreading my legs he positioned to enter me. I noticed I was aching and waiting excitingly for him to come in. I closed my eyes.

As he entered into me, my body was tight-it's been four months yoh! He kept whispering profanities… asking me how the sound of the ocean is pleasing to me… how lovely the stars are shining above me… how the cold breeze was caressing my body…before I knew-He was fully inside of me and began thrusting slowly… slowly… telling me how sweet I am, how this is more than he dreamed I would be and he increased the momentum… when his mouth touched my nipple again… something went loose inside of me… I started chanting and ranting… he went on faster and faster…one moment his mouth was on my nipple… The next minute he went sucking and licking my ear lobes… as he continued thrusting harder and deeper and faster… when he moved his hips in circular motions… I was sure my screams would wake everyone at the hotel… and he kept telling me

"Scream my baby… release yourself… ride with me"

Like the expert that he is, he turned me to my left, legs closed together, still buried deep within me and continued thrusting- I was panting like a dog thirsty for water… he fondled my breast, bent forward and had my right nipple in his mouth. He rode on… and on… and on.

He repositioned me on my back…. Held on to my tiny waist and fired away… I was fully with him now. Riding waves upon waves on ecstasy.

Then he stopped…. Lied on his back and asked me to come on top of him… as I slid down on his powerhouse sitting on him, my whole inside became full of him, and I began to ride… as I did… I began to feel goose pimples going off all over my body… as my breast danced in full view of his face

At the front of my veejayjah… just a few inches inside at the top… I felt a sweet sensation running through and it spread to my spine…. Such beautiful feeling! I leaned forward… wanting to tease that spot a little, as I did that… heavens let loose. I wasn't the naïve house wife anymore… no more the sexually inexperienced mother of seven…

I was a twenty six year old lady… enjoying sex for the first time in her life. And also for the first time in nine years of having sex, am very close to having an orgasm…my first orgasm… I rode on hard… and fast. I positioned myself at strategic points and was in control… screaming, panting… pinching Ernest… pulling my hair… holding my breast… I could feel it coming… then Ernest sat up… held my hips and continued thrusting hard and deep into me… his mouth went to my nipples and sucked and licked…

I climbed and climbed… by now I was deaf… I couldn't hear anything for a brief moment… and it happened… this sweet, indescribable feeling running all through my body… my brain… my heart… my every nerve shook and vibrated… and then it stopped. I collapse and was still. Very still! Ernest had to check up on me… Slowly I began getting emotional but remained silent. Ernest came shortly and I slept off immediately- into a very deep sleep…

5am…following day.

I woke up to this funny sensation running straight to my brains. It was Ernest's mouth working its magic on my nipple.

The fore play went on and on, it was like it lasted forever and when he began making love to me for real, I was all wet and ready- now a little bit experienced in the act.

I jump to my favorite horse-riding position and rode us to ecstatic bliss. Hmmm… to think that as at last night I didn't have a favorite sex position.

We slept a few minutes more and I headed straight home-after showering of course.

7am… following day!

Am lying in bed, lost in thoughts…before I go further…sorry about the explicit way with which I described this but I just want my ever pretentious Nigerian women to know that it's not that same thing they do only at night under the covers that I experienced. This was so much more. I know a lot women will castigate and say why say all this things? And ask all those moral questions. Well am telling my story and if I don't make you understand in detail what I am talking about, why bother talk about me? I know I am already been judged and some people are set to cast the first stone, if not already throwing deadly missiles my way.

Before you judge me, walk the road I have walked and see if you would do better than me.

I have now come to realize that a lot of women were like me. Ignorant of what they are missing out on and its funny how they turn their eyes away, not wanting to know the truth. To them if they don't know what they are missing, how can they care? Also they are those who know how this feels, but covers it up. And when we deny ourselves of our sexuality it leads to a whole of issues. We have to realize that we do have needs. We have desires and it's not a shame to enjoy sex. There's no law that forbids a woman from enjoying her sexuality. Why do we then deprive ourselves? I learnt mine through the wrong route. Am not proud of it but I want you to know that I am not alone on this journey. I know very well the consequences that come with adultery and I am smart to play my game well. I have seven small responsibilities but God knows I also need some tender love and care. I am not made of wood. Why do we continue to deprive ourselves? Why can't we wake up and embrace sex as God intended it.

I know loads of women are married but emotionally divorced so it's going to be quite an issue to feel anything for your hubby, especially when you know he is cheating on you with countless women. When was the last time you were affectionate with your hubby? When was the last time, he gave you a hug, a kiss perhaps? A kind word? Shown you appreciation? When was the last time he courted you? We are made to feel guilty to even bear the thought of a night out with our hubby. It's like our lives are defined before us. And those of us who are twenty-four hours on duty-call as full time housewives end up losing our identities and end up with very low self-esteem. We lose touch with who we are and end up feeling sorry for ourselves and all we can do is nurse our wounds in private.

Look at me today. Look deep into my story and notice the challenges that could be avoided and try to raise your daughters to grow up and be in control of their sexual lives. They ought not to be buried; they need to be in sync with their sexuality. Now I wished, only if my mother has taught me differently. But I guess she is also ignorant. Some people learn on their own, yes but please what about those who are not aware? Look at the culture we grew up with-the woman is made to look at sex as dirty. Even the bible shows that women should enjoy sex. The book, songs of Solomon is the perfect example.

Am not trying to make you see reason or justify my action; my personal choices which in this case is wrong, but right now as I speak I care less... it's my life and my decision. I have made my choice and I am living with it. This new adventure into the world of sexual excitement I have no single remorse about. I do not intend whatsoever to repeat this now or in the near future. God knows, am turning twenty–six how can I go on the next thirty years like this? The thought sickens me but I know it's a cross I have to bear, if for anything I need to maintain a good moral profile just for the sake of my kids. As tempting as the sexual escapade was; it's never going to happen a second time Period!

And to think the way chief goes about travelling like he doesn't expect me to want it is so very annoying. The few times he is home, the attitude with which he does it!! Like I was bought for that, I could be a vibrator for all he cares...yes a female vibrator. He doesn't undress me, he has never fondled my boobs, just very painful squeezes like he wants to tear it in two...*rolling eyes*. I have to seat chief down and have a heart to heart with him. This cannot go on. I will have to speak up, else I will die in this misery.

I won't and will never regret marrying chief. The sole purpose of my marriage was to cater for my family of seven and chief has fixed and positioned my brother's for life. They are all happily married and have happy and well cared for kids. That's thanks to me. Although every marriage has its own burdens and crosses, mine is sexual unfulfilment, lack of affection and of course "NO LOVE" and that is a dangerous combination for a woman. Even God knew how he wired us and warned our hubbies to love us.

It's kind of fortunate that I am circumcised. It is believed that the circumcised female does not get easily aroused and has a very low to nonexistent libido. It's also to my advantage that I had no time, early in life to attend a university. If I had attended the university I would have been exposed to a lot of things earlier. And after marriage I was the introverted type who was busy taking fabulous care of my half a dozen and one kids, I didn't have time to develop real friendships

Everyone saw the fabulous life I live and they never get to wonder about sex. And that ignorance is one of the issues affecting women mostly. Our views on sex have been altered.

If I could fall for this, I mean Ernest's sexual wooing with all my strict training and upbringing; it's hard to think of what ladies with low morals would do. Am very well behaved in all I do. I am the perfect daughter and sister. Can't say much for wife now as that file as been dented for life, like I was saying, if I could fall for this, be an adulterer with my strict foundation, think about those wild-eyed young married ladies and women out there.

Yes, you are already painting me black, but look at that cousin of yours, who you all thought wouldn't get married because she was wild and couldn't get her hands off men. The one caught in the act at age fourteen been humped by a man thirty years her senior, and had three abortions before the age of twenty-yes that cousin who partied all night and sleeps all day.

So, she was lucky to have met a rich guy like chief at age twenty-nine and the wealth and glam life blinded her, she didn't care if he was thirty years older when they first met. Going around town in exotic cars, living the luxury life was all that counted.

The times she was with chief before they were married, she was the sex machine- very wild and enjoyed sex to the maximum. All chief had to bring to bed was his growing mid-section and she was more than happy to do the rest, she didn't mind the pot belly, almost sagging breast. She loved sleeping at exotic and very expensive hotels, traveling to Dubai, London, Paris at first was a world too good to be true, after six to eight months of fantasies exploited plus the help of that Alfa at the Bar beach, chief paid her dowry.

At the same time business was so good, he was never around. After six months to one year of marriage… it has finally donned on your cousin.

You see, sex is a very private thing. We from this part of the continent are shy to discuss it and we protect it with all dignity. But the truth I have come to discover is that when you mature, just the way your body desires food and water, that's the way it makes demands on sex. You can't ignore your body when it cries for it-that's when you do enjoy it. I never cared before.

Now will your cousin fare better? Will she not long for that sweet, sensational love making by a strong able bodied man, now don't get me wrong, they are men out there above their fifties who have a dangerously high libido and they even take injections every twenty-one days to keep their libido high. Ernest told me about such injections yesterday.

Since your cousin's hubby happens to be the type who relaxes and let her do the work, then she is in for it. After all that is the tool she used to catch his attention, now that he has paid her dowry, he expects nothing less. He expects it all the time, whenever he demands. Its how you make your bed, you lie on it. Will a sexually active young woman just sit and watch her life go by? One who has tasted the sweetness of it and is not naïve like I had been. The naïve and religious ones will sit tight and bear in silence, but can the wild do it? Can they? But I tell you a large amount of people are doing selfish things behind the curtains to satisfy their sexual needs.

That widow at forty, who has spent twenty-two years in marriage, married to a highly sexed man who makes love to her four times a week. And gives her maximum satisfaction. Now that he is dead where does she begin from? And it's funny how people don't talk about that other aspect. They somehow expect the woman to have super powers and just cope without sex. They expect her to just switch off the button of her desires as a human being. Am not saying women should be prostitutes or be promiscuous, but my cry is that Africans especially Nigerians should acknowledge the fact that women have blood flowing through their veins too; they have sexual desires.

Even the wife of an imprisoned man was expected to stay without sex and be faithful to her husband and her marital vows for upward three decades. Marriage is for better, for worse right? I watched a movie of her life and saw how she was coldly treated. I don't know if there were other reasons to their decisions but my focus is on the sexual aspect. They were shocked that she should be with a man. They didn't even catch her red-handed. It was just speculations. And they crucified her. And these very same people, some can't stay two weeks without reaching for a means to cool off. At night when no man is there, do these widows not indulge in some sort of self-satisfaction! Doesn't she masturbate? Does she not sneak out at night or let some one in at the middle of the night?

And your mother, yes... you, your sexy size ten mother, who people never agree that she's your mum, now that she's separated from your dad or widowed- how does she satisfy her urge? As I speak you cringe. You don't want to know the details or the answer to that but hello?? Your mum is a human being. And she needs satisfaction. Think of it this way. See yourself at her age no longer sexually active... oh ho!!! You see? She shouldn't be scared to date or feel like she's letting you down because she feels horny just like you do. She's all flesh too girlfriend!

We should wake up and tell ourselves the truth. If our time is past and nothing can be done, we should begin now to imbibe the right wisdom on sex education into our daughters. Mother's should do the right thing. Now I have a daughter and I am going to do right by her.

One of the decisions I have taken is to discuss with chief to start an initiative for me where I can go to higher institutes and educate girls on sex. You??!! Yes me...who else better than me. I have been on the two sides of the fence and will use my terrible experience to any advantage. What about Ernest? You ask. Well like I earlier stated we know what we did. And we know where we are going. No matter the joy I derived from this I can never put the life of my seven children at stake because of personal pleasures.

I know many women are doing same for their kids. We endure different challenges and make different sacrifice-For the sake of our children. I don't know how life with chief will be, in ten or twenty years. I definitely can not foresee the future but one thing I know is; I am going to use this experience however negative it is to do the right thing. I am going to do my bit. Wherever you are. If you are a mother, an aunty, a school teacher, a grandmother and you read this and you have a little princess in your life that is budding and showing a lot of promise. Please I beg you, do right by her, teach her the things she should know-Guide her and educate her. Let her know her femininity is nothing to be ashamed about. I have said my bit, now...you do your part!

Hugs,

Chika....

STORY 3

Banke's Story

My name is Banke, this is not my story. But I am somewhat in the middle of it all. It's a story that's very rare to come by. One that's not what we usually hear about every day. Nor one of those our home videos try to portray about our lives as Nigerians. No. This is very different. And as I speak I don't know how to place it- If it's morally right or wrong! But things happen. And when they do, it's up to us to study the mistakes of whomever and pick up the good points from the story. The mistakes, we should try to avoid and the strong points we should strive to emulate. The typical Nigerian is cynical. It flows in their blood stream. It's a part of their psyche. The reluctance to look at things and issues 'realistically' is a big challenge and a threat to changes in our way of life. We should stop being rigid and try to relax and be flexible. Let's open up our minds to the endless possibilities all floating around us. There's so much changes going on all over the world-positive changes; we should go with the flow. Am telling this tale because it revolved somehow around me. And I witnessed all that happened, firsthand. My prayer is you pick a lesson or two.

I am a new mother living outside the shores of Nigeria, but born and bred in Nigeria. My hubby and I have just been blessed with a set of twins for our first attempt in child bearing. We have a boy and a girl. In every area of our lives, God has been good to us.

My own mother passed away at a tender age of twenty-nine. I grew up amidst aunties and uncles. My dad never remarried. My first real taste of a mother was when I met my boy friend now hubby, O.J's wonderful mother.

From day one when we officially began dating, O.J took our relationship very serious and He took me home to see his mother almost immediately. He is the last child and a mummy's boy in a loving kind of way.

The mum welcomed me with so much love and care that I was suspicious at first. You know, suspicious in the naija kind of way. How can someone be so selfless? My mum-in-law is an angel. She gave herself all in all in service to her family.

She has never worked-not a day in life, despite graduating from the university top of her class. I have no idea if it's a decision she made or it was imposed on her after marriage. She cooks-not just the normal everyday meal…but very excellent food. I always feel like am in a five star restaurant anytime I spend the weekends there. I love the way she serves her dishes. And she has very beautiful plates too. The presentation of the food on the plate is always mind blowing. No matter how small or irrespective of the type of food, you always see professionalism and the love and care she puts into every dish. She washes everything; dishes, clothes etceteras. I used to wonder how she coped with bringing up my hubby and siblings in those days when there were no washing machines. It must have really been stressful because what my hubby did with his first salary was make a down payment for a washing machine. She keeps her home squeaky clean. Her kitchen is always sparkling. Every item methodically arranged for easy access. When you look around her home, one thing stands out-this is no ordinary woman. Her intelligence and very effective mind shows with everything she does. She pampers her hubby and kids. She is hospitable; she welcomes everyone to her home. She's generous. She speaks gently and kindly. She always has a word of encouragement to dish out. A smile, a hug, I mean at first I was like – is she for real? She is my version of the Proverbs thirty-one wife.

But there was a snag to all of this. Yes-BUT! NOTHING IS PERFECT RIGHT? Well, I don't know if my experience of being motherless made me notice this situation faster but it screamed loud at my face-Day in, day out over the years. Whenever I visited my boyfriend, then fiancé, now hubby, I noticed that my Angelic mother-in-law was taken for granted by all. I don't know who I could say mistreated her the most; my hubby's siblings or the hubby, my father-in-law.

I watched year after year as my mother-in-law was treated like trash. Her daughters use her as a child care giver-a nanny. They leave the grand kids with her. Now there's nothing wrong there. But the shabby way they go about it. Like it's their right and not a privilege, amazes me. They never say thank you. No appreciation whatsoever. One can see it in their demeanor. They are cold to her. No affection. They never call after dumping the babies. They never stay back to chat when they return to pick their babies. They speak down at her, send her on errands. She does their cooking. Oh yes, you read right. They claim there's no need hiring a cook when their mum is idle. So the mum cooks for them weekly. Each of them takes home their own dishes, all properly packed separately. But they buy the groceries together.

When they are having a party, my mum-in-law is chef, baby sitter, steward, cleaner, all in one. They scream out orders like she was a paid help. All these she takes in with a smile.

Let's talk about my mama-in-laws sons. My hubby is the last child and the only one who stops to ponder on the needs of his mother. And I in the picture made sure he does exactly that. When I visit my mum-in-law wherever she goes for "Omugwo" (a Nigerian native word-pronounced OMUU GWOH! its where a mother visits her own daughter or daughter-in-law who just gave birth and spends anytime from three to twelve weeks caring for the new born baby) at any of her older sons house, am always depressed. Depressed at how low a child can debase his mother. And how my supposedly mates treat her unfairly. I told myself note to self – never to do same.

Point to note: My parents' in-law are of average income level. It's not like they are very rich. So, many times I wonder on the basis of their arrogance-unto what really?

Now it's my turn and I was so excited to receive my mother-in-law. Now I said 'was' because things have turned around to something unimaginable. I don't know whether to term this "Omugwo" a blessing or a curse.

How do I begin? How? I live in a luxurious estate in a posh part of Houston where my dear hubby is employed. We lived very comfortably with our over three hundred neighbors all doing excellently well and from all works of life.

Prior to my estimated date of delivery, we applied for visa for my Mother-in-law and she was given the customary two years visiting visa. She came over immediately.

I have never had my mother-in-law over at my house before. This was my first time to host her. I was super excited. From the airport where I went to pick her up, I knew I was in for a good time. Whoa!!! She brought bags and bags of Nigerian delicacies. I was elated. She brought different soups – afang, edikaikong, oha, egusi, ogbono, banga. She freeze them stove cold and brought them over. All six bowls of delicious soups, prepared by her. I was overjoyed. Where did she get the money to do all this? I asked. She said she sold some wrappers. God!!! Is she for real? This woman is an angel.

Another point to note: My mother-in-law is sexy!! I am not joking when I say sexy. She's got a flat tummy, a very beautiful face and her boobs are small and portable. Not bad at all for a sixty-five years old. She is a size twelve UK. You get the picture?

From the moment she stepped into my home, I was in heaven. Pure Joy! God!! Was this what it felt like? The love of a mother! What pure bliss I have missed out on all these years. Oh where do I begin from? Before I gave birth, this angel would wake me up in bed with freshly made fruit juice. She would run me a bath, seat by my bed and gist with me while I bathed.

This was after she must have cleaned the whole house sparkly clean. She stopped me from waking up early to clean and cook for my hubby before he left for work. Then after my bath, she would lie me down on my bed three times a week and massage the hell out of me. *Laughing*... pardon my language!! I can still feel my body relax under her expert fingers. Jeez! Did this woman go to massage school?

From the bedroom where I would lay down for a bit I would proceed to the kitchen to eat something usually delicious. She is so organized. She always held a small tet a tet before bed time. Asking me what and what I would love to be done the following day and also what shopping needed to be done. What clothes needed to be washed, which room should be vacuumed etc oh my God! This angel I would beg to run my life. She's excellent at it.

This went on smoothly till I gave birth to our twins. She was with me all through labor and birth. She was so dedicated to her duties. She gave me the customary hot baths of new mothers in Nigeria. Not all tribes in Nigeria practice this. But we hold it sacred. It's believed to help return the body back to shape and make the belle go back to size. We use almost boiling water to bath from our head to our toes. We don't fix hair extensions when it's time for delivery. All we have on is our natural hair. But it's a great help. Towels are dipped into very hot water, squeezed a little and pressed against our tummy. The towels are pressed in a downward motion.

I slept soundly not like a mother of twins. She refused to let me sleep in same room with my babies-as is practiced back home. She opted to do that. My sex life with my hubby jumped back on track because I was under no pressure. I don't know how she bathes the twins. They fall right to sleep after her expert fingers have done her magic on them.

Into the second month of my babies' birth, we began planning our babies' presentation to church. We were planning on using a hall that's owned by a fellow West African who also resides in our estate. We made calls and he came over. He is a bastardly rich widower with two grown up daughters and a teenage son. He is forty nine.

The babies' presentation came and we celebrated in style. My hubby and I noticed nothing strange.

Weeks after my babies' presentation, I sat alone one afternoon waiting for my Mother-in-law who went out for a stroll. I was bored and missing her, so I called her. She answered in her usual sweet voice. I could hear joyous laughter of youths on the background. Wondering, I asked where she was. She told me she was out shopping with Mr. X's kids. She wants to prepare them a meal. She went on to ask me if I needed anything. I said no and went on to explain that I was just checking up on her.

She returned several hours later. She was dropped off by Mr. X's kids and they spent another good twenty-eight minutes (yes twenty eight!!! I checked) chatting in my driveway. The last kid came down, gave her a big hug and ran back to the car. And they drove off.

I kept quiet. Things went on smoothly. Week after week I noticed my Mother-in-law changing. Great positive changes. She began visiting the gym in company of Mr. X's daughter-I must mention. She came home with bags after bags of new designer clothing's. She got a new hair do. She began wearing trendy make-up! Then the inner glow!! Wow!!

She glows!! She began looking rejuvenated. Sharper, smarter, and more agile! I noticed bounce to her steps. I noticed how very tender she has become. It's like her real nature sprang out. Her voice was a little higher than a whisper when she speaks. Love, joy, wisdom flows from within her you could touch it; I was happy and miserable the same time. She was radiating and oozing out confidence and a deep sense of contentment.

I watched in Awe, confused as to how to approach the issue. During our nightly tete-a-tete where we plan the next day ahead, I noticed three times a week – once during weekend. She spends three to four hours away from home, but she was so wise as to plan everything well. As in her schedule with the kids that I felt no lapses or strain.

This woman is a rare gem. She has topnotch organizational skill. She could effortlessly run an empire. She had a knack for perfection and whatever she sets her mind to do, she does it. By now, all my neighbors are in love with her. Who wouldn't? She would bake cookies and cupcakes and different mouth watering desserts as often as she could and send over to our neighbors. I shouldn't over look the fact that she goes there and delivers it herself.

It's been six months after the arrival of my mother-in-law. I was sure no one back home would have been able to recognize her. Even I in my late twenties struggle for a catch up with her. She was on point on all angles. Physically she was in top shape. Ha! Did I forget to mention she gets awards on weekly basis from her gym? I think from winning targets. She also made loads of friends from the gym who came over to our home. I watched in awe as she laughs and chats away so contented with her friends from gym who cuts across different continents of the world. I wasn't surprise to hear her welcome her Indian friend in her Indian dialect "Namaste" with both palms crossed or when I hear her say "Danke" to her Deutshe friend over the phone. She was learning different foreign dialect. French was a piece of cake. She makes three to four sentences fluently.

Mentally, she was sound as I also noticed she gets two books every week we go shopping. A big one and a small one. She reads four big books and four small one in a month! And that is not all; she buys audio Cd's and DVD's like they are going extinct. Spiritually to me this woman is going to heaven. No speed breakers on her way. No curves or bends or bad spots. She's heading to heaven 100km/ph. She now heads the senior league in our church. She looks so out of place amongst those old fragile people. She is the president of the women's club that is from South-South Nigeria. She's got so many bright ideas for the end of year festival. I don't know what she has introduced to the seniors She presides over in church here. They all begin to look well kept and full of life. They hold weekly meetings at alternate homes. They are yet to come to my home. Up on till then, I don't know what the meeting is all about. But with my Mother-in-law. I have high hopes.

Financially – she gets allowances from my hubby. And due to her superfine method of housekeeping. I have learnt to be prudent in managing money. My home is stocked to full capacity. I have learnt how to be patient in shopping. How to compare products, and get the best deals out of everything. For the past three months I have not touched a dollar out of my monthly allowance. Not because I am trying to be frugal but honestly I have no space to store groceries, provisions and other household necessary items. Am fully stocked. Out of appreciation, I gave her a full month's allowance.

She also gets all paid for cooking for Mr. X and tutoring Mr. X's last child – His only son. In her selfless nature, she went shopping for her grand kids back in Nigeria. She shopped for each child's every need. Toys, clothes, books, shoes, tooth paste, supplements, etc. and shipped to Nigeria.

Socially, she's A – okay. She attends functions regularly. Most times I tag along more out of curiosity. I always get VIP treatments whenever I tag along. It's like she's a governor's wife or a wife of a highly placed Nigerian citizen back home. She is always called upon to give a speech or a short talk. Boy, she always brings tears to the eyes of those listening to her. At the end of her speeches, everyone in the room is dying to shake hands with this royalty. My Mother-in-law, who only months ago was living an average life in Nigeria. Riddled by endless meaningless chores and surrounded by loveless people, who trampled on her personality.

Overall, she was doing amazingly well. After the goods were received in Nigeria, I started getting calls, Impatient and derogatory calls. It was one daughter after another, then the sons joined in, then the son's wives who were my mates but by far my seniors, then my father-in-law. Hell was let loose… They needed to know when their mother and wife will return to her 'duties' in Nigeria. Note I said 'duties'. I never heard one child say I missed my mother. All I heard were impatient and rude remarks of how their mother is unfaithful to her duties. The grand kids are lacking care. The bills they are paying for child care is such a waste when they have a jobless mother.

The sons also had their say, especially the one whose wife just put to birth her sixth child. He was so furious because the mum should be there to care for his wife and the kids. Why did I claim her as if she is my property? He asked me. I spoke to my hubby about the pointless insults. He in turn called his mum and asked her when she would want to return. Three times he approached her, three times she said nothing. My hubby was worried, being that he was home only at nights and most times out of trips. He didn't notice much.

I got the message clear that Mother-in-law had no plans in returning to the hell which she came from. I was touched. I, on the one hand selfishly admitting the truth would not want her away from me. She has made my life so easy and fun. She is a friend, a confidant; she is my prophetess, my nurse, the best granny to my kids.

My hubby called my attention to the issue at hand; I couldn't come out with the little I knew, so I kept mum. She had to return home, her ticket had been adjusted once, now it's almost time for the new date. He said something must be done. The father needs his wife (Needs his slave – you mean!!) Humph!! – I thought to myself silently.

Much later that night, I decided to talk to my Mother-in-law. I politely asked to speak with her privately. She obliged. We went into the guest room.

"Mama … you are the only mother I have ever known"… I stated "And in this past few months I have grown to love you like I would my own mother. But Ma, you came here for a reason. And its time for you to return, to your duties as a wife. You have a life and a home you left back in Nigeria. You left people that needs you. The pressure is hot on my hubby, and I have also gotten my fair share of false accusations."

"My hubby told me that thrice he has called you about your departure and thrice you kept mute all through the conversations – if it can be called that. Mama, please what is the issue or challenge here? At least speak to me. I may not be advanced in age, but I am growing. I am a woman, a mother and can at least relate to you and try to see things from your angle. Please ma, silence will take us nowhere. No matter how difficult it may be for you, please express your concern and we will know how to tackle it... please."

She kept quiet for a long time. I struggled not to check my phone for time or look at the clock on the wall. I watched her expressionless face- I couldn't read any emotion. I looked at her countenance, her body was stiff. Her shoulders squared. She sat upright. Legs crossed. Her gaze faced upwards to the ceiling. She could be mistaken for someone with a stance for battle. She looked like someone boiling on the inside, like someone who is ready for a fight. Her frequent signs of hmmm and hissing plus nodding her head confirmed that all is not well indeed.

My mind flew to Mr. X, could he have a hand in this? The closeness between them had grown; her bond with the kids has also grown stronger. I wondered if there was more to this whole saga.

"My daughter…" Mother-in-law spoke.

I was shocked, and brought out of my wandering thoughts. Part of me had accepted that she would be non-responsive and keep me quiet just the way she had my hubby.

"I am not going to say much"… she continued.

I nodded my head in acknowledgement. For me, anything would suffice. We just needed to know what was wrong and if possible, fix it. Asides the fact that we were under pressure for her return back home, we were first and foremost concerned for her well being.

"Mama … Am all ears!" I whispered, afraid if I spoke loud enough that she could change her mind.

"Am going to ask you two (2) questions"…she said

"okkaayy!!"… I responded slowly, almost scared to speak.

She continued "Go back to who?"

"Secondly, go back to what?" she asked with her brows lifted… urging me to reply her.

"Haa! Haaaa!" I replied in shock. "Your husband, your kids and your home now mama!!"

"Hmmmm??" She began shaking both knees and head simultaneously…. "Hmmmmm????"

"Was that a question?" I wondered, not daring to speak out! This hmmm's are becoming too frequent for comfort.

"Husband eh? Husband? My daughter you said husband?" she asked.

"Yes ma" I responded … what else could I say? I continued "You need to go back to your home. Your older kids need you mama!"

"Older kids? You mean the thirty plus, forty plus and almost fifty plus kids I have? Are those the kids you are talking about my daughter?"

"Hmmm" I was shocked to see that I have also started saying 'hmmm'

"Yes ma" I said almost ashamed of myself

"Okay…" she responded. She became suddenly calm. Her eyes lit up like she has got the solution to the problem that has been eating her away.

"See …" she began "Please tell my husband and the so-called kids that I have no intention whatsoever to return to Nigeria. Not to talk of go back to that house!"

I jumped up. And fell straight and hard on my knees "mama Please"

"Why"… I asked

"Please"…I begged

"Why?" I cried

"Am through with talking" she stood up to leave, then sat back as if having second thoughts.

"My dear! Go and call me my son … tell him to come with a tape recorder or any gadget that can record what I have to say. I do not intent to repeat myself after this night."

I jumped to my feet and hurried back to my hubby's room to get him. I barged in, woke him up and quickly filled him in on the newest development.

"What?! She can't be serious!!" He barked, jumped out of bed and walked past me, heading straight for the guest room.

I stood back and said a quick silent prayer, then ran after him. Hell was about to break loose and it's about to, right under my roof.

"God! Please take control"…I prayed in a whisper, then followed slowly.

I walked in. Hubby was interrogating his mother. She kept mute. We both sat down. She obviously was in no rush to speak.

"Mum"

"Mum… am here now! Sorry about how I first screamed at you. I am here now please do speak up!"

"Where is the tape recorder?"

"Here Ma! I can do that with my phone". He said

"Okay" she said "I am ready to speak"

"Press play"

"This is your wife and your mother speaking. I presume you are all seated to hear me speak. Firstly, I want to say thank you to the Man who answered the name Husband for forty plus years of my life ..." she went on and poured her mind

Then she was done.

"Please go back home and play the tape, you people should hurry and work out something. Time is of the essence."

My hubby couldn't stand to his feet. It was as if he was paralyzed. I too, was in shock. My darling kept looking at me, silently searching for answers.

Two days later, found us back in Nigeria-in my father-in-laws parlor. And of course they rained insults on us as to the absence of their mother.

What are you going to say is the reason for your mother not been here? ...

Question followed question. My mates were given me hard stares! Questionable looks.

"This woman has a responsibility to our father! She is married! Did she forget that? Her grandkids that she baby-sits have all been under duress and she sits and whiles away precious time?" That was the eldest son speaking.

"This woman?"... My hubby asked calmly "you mean our mother?"

The eldest son shot him a murderous look

"Okay! Okay!! Okay!!!"...chipped in my papa-in-law. "We are all seated. Please let's not be in a hurry. We are here like you requested!"

"I don't think the wives and hubbies should be here, I mean our in-laws. This is a sensitive and highly delicate matter that should not be heard by another except our immediate family. If word gets out, it could be disastrous!"... My hubby said calmly, still quite shaken. He hasn't slept since the night his mother shocked our socks off.

"Meaning? Look at this small boy! Meaning? Meaning what now? Are you saying your wife is ignorant of the reason we are all seated here? Is that it?" Fired the eldest daughter.

"Suit yourselves and NOTE! I told you so" my hubby replied.

He stood up and dropped the phone on the table and pressed play.

Seconds later.........

Her calm, sensational voice filled the room; this woman could pass for a world renowned speaker and teacher. When she speaks, you are commanded to listen. I mean you are spell bound.

"This is your wife and mother speaking. I presume you are all seated to hear me speak. Firstly, I want to say thank you to the man who answered the name husband for forty plus years of my life…"

My gazed shifted to my father-in-law… He shifted uncomfortably in this favorite couch. His toes, twitching in anxiety.

"I send greetings from the land of milk and honey. Not to dwell too much on frivolities, am going straight to the point". She paused.

"You all, I am presuming are expecting me back or rather are of the opinion that I should be there now fulfilling the duties of my dowry (money paid on a woman before marriage according to the traditional laws and customs of the region of Africa they originate from) was paid for. I know Chike my eldest son by now would be wondering where "This woman" has got the guts to hold back from her matrimonial duties. Yes Chike, this woman has finally grown some wings "This woman" you all affectionately called me, has grown some livers."

"This woman" was an "A straight" student who did exceptionally well in school with the hope of going further. "This woman" had dreams and goals and wanted to fulfill her destiny like any woman would long for. Yes, any woman, even the un-kept one, whose lazy ass can't play or fulfill her role as a mother but keep popping out children like its going out of fashion. Yes you -wife of my eldest son, who fondly call me "This woman".

"This woman" has given nothing but one hundred percent pure love same undiluted devotion to caring for you all. As you grew, I did the best I could, but I guess laziness is hereditary on the paternal side of the family. Laziness, arrogance, no morals, shabbiness, and no spiritual base or refusal to acknowledge God, I could go on. "This woman" strived to make out something from your life, but "This woman" ultimately failed because probably fate is at work"

"Every passing day "This woman's" heart bled from anguish just to wake up to meet the kids and hubby my world resolves around. Constant disappointment banged at the door of my heart. I felt Knife piercing agony, to watch the kids I strived to make something out of their lives, turn out to be indigents."

"My sons grew to be lazybones-my sons!! From my womb! Indolent! Slothful! Mean! It couldn't be true. Every day, I felt disappointed to wake up to the realization that I bore failures, instead of world changers. For years, I blamed myself because I thought maybe I didn't try harder or probably the prayer sessions I had then when you kids were little, weren't enough. Due to this self accusation and deep guilt for bringing failures into this world, I struggled to serve harder, to try and make your lives better".

"But the more I laid out my life to serve you, the more I noticed violent displays of bitterness, anger and all worth not. I toiled to make your homes better. My daughters turned out to be everything short of my heart desire. Women that are not capable of running their own homes. I cooked their meals from my own pot. I took great care of the kids for them. Even to bath your own kids properly, you can't. Astute laziness, willing laziness, constant and chronic procrastination has eaten deep into the bones of you all. Lateness to everything! God, I hate been late! While on the other hand, you and your kids derive great pleasure in been late or arriving the latest to every occasion or event. Even the events, that promises to change your lives for the better".

"I enabled you all. I was an enabler. You all need a wakeup call. And this is it; my days of slaving for you are over. And by God, this step I am taking is long overdue. If a grown ass man cannot do his own monthly shopping at forty years plus and the woman he calls his wife can't do the duties she was married to play in his life, I am saying today with deep EMPHASIS: Please get ready to go HUNGRY!! NO more 'This Woman' go get us this things".

"Now to the more important issues; my marriage to your father. My dear hubby, as for my marriage to you. How do I begin? For years I wept at night, in my own privacy. Watching my life go slow before me, watching the days creep by, the rising and the setting sun, each day arose with its share of blessing but all I could ever achieve in each passing day was been an extension of your lives-yes, you all I mean".

"You married me with so much promise; you saw all the good in me, all the talents, the skills, the ambition and the will to live a fabulous life. You took me in then KILLED IT! Yes, you succeeded in killing it by relegating it to the background. You intentionally drove me far away from anything that will keep me in the path of pursing my purpose in life. To you, my purpose was to serve you. Yes, but not as selfishly as you carved it out to be. Now am here. I see the light at the end of the tunnel! I am turning sixty-six (66)"

"I married you as a virgin. You ravaged my body from the tender age of sixteen to the next twelve years of my life. At age twenty-eight, you began neglecting me and the six kids. You ran off from your responsibilities. Sex was vague, but it was what brought us within meters of each others. It was the only thing that showed intimacy. I never knew orgasm with you. But I knew it's a possibility. You were selfish and self-centered. You ravaged my young body, then you dumped it. From age twenty eight to forty eighty. You only slept with me like once in every six months, it graduated to once in one year, then to once in two years before you stopped completely."

"I have not had sex-Yes sex! For the last eighteen years. hahahahahah!! Wicked being! At the age of forty-eight, you abandoned me for life. That was supposed to be the end of my sexual journey right Mr.? That was how I would have gone to my grave; sexually unfulfilled and frustrated. You didn't care what I think. You didn't care how I fared. You didn't stop to think about me as a human being. Not that I was not physically fit. I was in great shape and always took excellent care of my body, but NO! My dear hubby preferred running after his daughter's age mates and fulfilling all his sexual fantasies"

"What stopped you from having fun and also exercising your conjugal duties? This is Africa, did you forget? I have no single say in that! You are free to do as you wish. You are permitted to sleep with as much women as you like, marry as many women as you want to. I can't utter a word. Our society and culture has given you guys the go ahead. But you chose to punish me, WHY? You sentenced me to a life of loneliness and rejection. A life where the very core of me, ached for years- yearning for your touch. A life where I was scared. My heart ached second after second in anguish. I was a living dead. A walking corpse. Why all the wickedness? For all the good I brought to your life, you choose to treat me badly".

"Hmmmmm… but today all I can say to you is-thank you! My dear husband and ungrateful children. I have shocking news for you all today. In the past few weeks….I threw caution to the wind. I asked myself a simple question; if I happen to be on my death bed today, what would I have done differently. I am turning sixty-six. And am closer to the grave than ever. I decided to be selfish for the first time in my life and have a taste of the good life. I put morals and religion aside and made a selfish decision. One that I have been surprise I feel no single guilt about. I let go my moral compass and took a bite from the forbidden apple".

"There's a young chap here who's forty-nine, a widower and very much interested in me. I don't care if its love but the chemistry is mutual. It was so strong that I gave in to his persistent advances- his petting, his sweet and affectionate words. The ways he courted me, pampered me, he appreciated me has been mind-blowing. He understood and listened to me. His children adored me. Yes, I could be their grandma but these kids stirred something deep within me; their level of focus gladdens my heart. The way they are humble despite the fact that their father is a millionaire in all currencies. With him, I felt like a woman for the first time in years and I fell-I gave in. Few months back I let him make sweet, erotic, passionate love to me. He made love to me almost on a daily basis. We couldn't get enough of each other. The past month I made love twenty-six days out of thirty! Even I was amazed I could keep up. I think it's all the years of been deprived that has accumulated and had given me a high drive. He made me feel very young and wanted."

"Haaaaaaaaaaaa!!! My heart!!!! My heart!!!!"-that was my father-in-law gasping for air, his right hand on his left side squeezing hard while slumping to the floor.

My hubby rushed to put off the recorder, for a brief moment.

"Papa!! Papa!!! Papa!!!! – The children screamed, running round him to pick him up.

I tiptoed near to find him not moving. He laid motionless and stiff. Fear crept into my heart.

One of the children brought cold water and poured on him. And he sprang up in shock. They consoled him. He began sobbing, first quietly, like one trying to convince himself that all he just heard was not real. Then when realization dawned on him that he indeed heard right. The sobbing increased in intensity and he began waving his head from side to side, tapping his feet hard on the floor – saying "God! God!!! What have I done? What have I done?"

Please switch on the recorder let me hear all...

We all went back to our sitting positions. Every one of them dazed. Listening to her twice didn't remove the element of shock. I too felt chaotic inside. I look at my husband and he looked confused and scared too. This was a huge problem on ground. Very huge. My hubby switched it back on...

Mama's voice continued...

"My body is rejuvenated. Love making and the constant orgasmic heights I am been taken to constantly has made me whole. To think that such heights existed. My hubby may God punish you!! So this is what you deliberately deprived me of? With all the neglect and wicked vices of yours, you could at least have had mercy and fulfilled my sexual desires. Then I would know that even in all my misery I had one good thing to look forward to. But it was not to be. It's clear you had no feeling for me. Even one can't do such great wicked to his enemy. There should be a limit to your inhumane treatments. I tried and tried in my teenage age to help you help us - you refused. You never wanted foreplay, you never wanted lubrication. I was sore and constantly in pains from your barbaric treatments and rough sex you enjoyed. I am sure even animals do better. How you could derive pleasure in all my pains, supersedes me".

"Today's story is different! I now Glow… I live. I am alive. As I write, the very core of me tingles with delight, with fulfillment."

"Am finished! Am finished!! God, I am finished!!!" – Papa-in-law chipped in.

The recording played on without interruption….

"But that is not all!"

"There's more???…. Jesus!!!" Papa-in-law sang, now visibly shaken.

She continued uninterrupted

"After months of been away from your enslavement my real persona began to slowly resurface. I began to feel the real me. I woke up delighted to see a new day. I take long walks and look around the beautiful surrounding and bask in the sweet aura of it all. I go to sleep with so much peace, have sweet dreams and wake up with great optimism to face a new day. I have been depressed for so long as a result of being verbally abused by you my kids, and your dear father, my husband. I was emotionally neglected, emotionally abused, sexually frustrated to the core, under valued, rejected daily, physically drained and exhaustedly worn out and faded plus mentally handicapped. I thought my Life was written off!"

"Today the story is different. I would risk all never return to the hell I call marriage or home."

"Now these are my decisions and I expect you all to honor it!

1. I am never returning to Nigeria, even when I die, I demand to be buried here.
2. I would want the dowry paid on my head, according to the native law and customs of our land to be returned. You all are all married. Your father and I have no joint duty together anymore as Man and wife. Also, I have crossed the line. And if things are not done right on time it will be disastrous to everyone. We all know how our ancestors frown upon

adultery-no matter the issues that lead to it. So please take care of that aspect traditionally.

3. I don't intend to marry again and I don't think that I am in love. No, I am just me. Feeling free and appreciated here for been me. The things I do for you people that you termed inadequate, have earned me positions in high places here. I am finally worth something. I am finally contributing my quota to life; even at sixty six it's not too late".

"So dear ones… you can assume I am dead! After this, if you feel so much ashamed, I would give you total support if you tell everyone back home that I am DEAD!!! Pleeeeaaassseee I beg you!! I need a fresh lease on life. A fresh start. I want to end my days enjoying what little is left of my life. I want to wake up with optimism and sleep with fulfillment from new friendships and the new bonds I have built here. The love and acceptance I enjoy are priceless, so whatever you decide… decide fast! I go off now. Thanks for your time"

"Thuunddd!!!" That was the sound of my father-in-law's body as he fell hard to the floor again, fainted.

They revived him again and suggested they take him to see a doctor.

He fainted again…

We got him into a car and drove to the hospital. During the drive to the hospital I wondered silently…"what's all this fainting about? Seriously! Why this fainting spells? Until some few months ago "This woman" meant nothing to him. Imagine not sleeping with a woman for eighteen years straight… how can he? When he is busy chasing after small girls round town. Sincerely speaking, one of my prayer points is for my dearly beloved hubby not to end up like his dad. This man can womanize!!! God!!! He is so Randy! And judging by the way my dearly beloved hubby does not joke with sex; I know he got his high libido and stamina from his dad. Sometimes…. no-many times I have wondered what would happen when I can no longer keep up with his demands. Will he stray like his father?

Well, back to what's on ground… my papa-in-law has been crying non-stop. He is inconsolable. He was placed under observation for his blood pressure went up drastically.

I try to guess what actually is killing him here. Is it the fact that someone has been romping his advanced wife? Or the fact that, the wife is not returning to him; to take over her slave duties.

"This woman" has watched him womanize with girls his daughter's age. She has endured all the lies when he mysteriously disappears at night. The fake trips out of town, the refusal to pick his calls… he won't even believe when he sees Mother-in-law. She's so beautiful now and she glows. She's is filled with life.

I don't know how these guys are going to go about this. I look at them all, from one ungrateful wretch to the other…thank God they can't hear my thoughts….

The whole family is silent, everyone has gone dumb. I had half expected that by now, they would be hurling insults at my hubby for taking their mother to the land of freedom and had the scales fall from her eyes. But to my greatest surprise, everyone is silent! All rooted deep in thoughts, looking from one to the other, in total confusion.

"How do we handle this?"… At long last someone spoke.

By now, we were all seated around the hospital bed of my papa-in-law.

"I can't live without my wife"… papa-in-law chipped in… Sobbing bitterly… "These past months have been hell".

"Hell? How?" Asked, my hubby "How? Tell us? I for one thought her absence would have given you all the chance you need to womanize to your heart's desire…"

"My son …" started papa-in-law.

"Don't my son me papa…" continued my hubby "you played your role in what has led us to this moment. I knew mama was persevering, but I didn't know you were torturing her emotionally, physically, psychologically, financially in fact three hundred and sixty degrees she was in hell. Now look! See? See now?? How do we correct this?"

"I will die oh!! I will die oh!! I need my wife back please... I will die oh!!"

"See Papa... Mama has a point. A lot of water has passed under the bridge. Assuming we are even able to convince her to stay put in the marriage. How do we appease our ancestors? You know the customary law here ... when a woman sleeps outside with one or several men while the dowry of her hubby is still on her head, she has defiled the family altar. It's a taboo, an abomination. The only remedy is to appease the ancestors of this family... How do we go about that?"

"Haaa!!"... God help me!! ...Haaa!!..." papa-in-law continued crying... "We will serve the gods oh! I need my wife back oh!"

"Papa... it's not as easy as you say it oh! Have you thought of the ridicule? The......"

"Ridi... what!!!! ... Ridicule what?? ... O.J are you saying because two or three persons will sit down and gossip. Gossip about my foolishness and your mums shocking decisions over drinks, laugh and make mockery of us, then go back to their homes and face their own realities, I should spend my old age alone? So because of that I should be afraid of ridicule????... Tell me"

He looked at all of them waiting for answers, then continued "And by the ways, why are you all quiet? Why is O.J the only one talking?"

"Papa ... it's enough!!" replied my hubby.

The others still quiet as can be.

My Papa–in-law, now calm continued speaking to my husband "Please make arrangement to sell my house at Lagos-Ibadan expressway...I believe it can fetch more than fifty million naira... sell it and let's get started O.J. I need an American visa please... I am relocating to the U.S"

"What?" Screamed everyone. Even I was taken unaware.....
"What??"

"What is the 'what' about?" he queried them

"I am asking?" said papa-in-law. "Did you buy the property with me? Oh! Okay. You were looking to inherit the land when I die right? It's a pity. And if it's about me relocating to meet my wife, please which one of you will volunteer to take care of me till old age…answer me? You almost poisoned me with your cooking these past months. Everything you cook, I see oil swimming on top everywhere! You call that cooking or you had plans to kill me? All this while we have been talking, you all kept quiet. Now I talk of relocating, you open your stupid mouths to shout what?"

He turned to my husband "Please my son O.J… Begin a search for a place. An apartment big enough for your mum to start a daycare. I know she would love that. Don't bother about the price. Just let me know when you find it. Also try and get information about running a daycare, all the necessities involved. But please ensure that the location is close to your place, since she has established her presence in the community. I wouldn't want to take her away from the people she loves so much and those things that have helped resuscitate her. Also begin preparations to apply for my visa. We are seniors, we shouldn't encounter any immigration issues. My decision to buy a house there should hold enough water right?"

"Papa … what if mama rejects you?" asked my hubby.

"She should be ready for a stalker because am not spending the rest of my life without my wife."

"O.J Please call her for me… tell her I will pay for all the wrong. I will love her with everything in me. We will explore sex together. We will go on trips together. We will both travel to see the world! God knows, I am ready to sell as much property as I need to raise the cash! I need my wife back! I will do anything; go any length to get this marriage back!! I won't stop!! I won't relent! From this moment this is my only mission. We will do all traditional rites to appease the gods on her behalf… yes we will. But live without my angel. It's a No NO!!!"

Mama-in-law vehemently refused at first. The hatred or bitterness had consumed her. But after listening to the tears of her hubby and the length he is willing to go… the sacrifice of spending the rest of their lives in Diaspora with a promise only to be returned when dead… Mother-in-law is finally listening.

She even agreed to come very briefly to do the traditional rites herself and get some other stuff she needs to travel with.

My husband's siblings, all spoke to her on Skype. They apologized profusely and wept bitterly. She forgave them and spoke sternly to them. Asking them to build their lives without her because now, she won't be there to carry their burdens.

Before we left, they call each other twice or thrice every day and from what I see, Papa-in-law is acting like a teenager in love. When we showed him her pictures, he shed tears. When we showed him videos of her dancing at parties, giving speeches and speaking to the seniors at church, he was completely shocked! He said he thought she had put all of that behind when they got married. He said he felt she has decided to focus on family and let go of that life. She never complained or said anything pertaining going back to school or pursuing a career or business. I know it sounds bland, but who am I to speak?

We got back to the states and did all we were asked to do. Mama was ecstatic about the daycare facility. She broke off her relationship with Mr. X, but I am sure they will remain friends for life-You don't forget people like that.

My father-in-law got his visa, but He insisted they travel a bit first before heading to the United States to begin their second phase of life. So my husband booked them Lagos-South Africa, South Africa-Dubai, Dubai-Hong Kong, Hong Kong-India, India-Dubai, Dubai-London(he got them a transit visa),finally London-Houston! It's going to be a ten weeks tour that will set my Papa-in-law back tens of thousands of dollars. But the old man doesn't care. I didn't know that average guy could wake up and be this romantic. I feel so jealous right now.

The 'serving of the gods' will take place a day before they leave. They kept it closely knitted as possible. Very few people they say would be aware of it.

I don't know how things will pan out but we are all hoping for the best.

So pick a lesson or two and try to avoid any such disasters before it happens. If a sixty-six years old woman can lose her guard, then watch how you treat that pretty thirty something wife of yours, you treat like trash. The one whom you sexually neglect for a year or two, without touching her. If you are so stupid to ply this route, you can never tell the disaster that's waiting to happen. And who knows, you may be the one to lose everything.

Also if you see your situation as one that nothing can be done to help you get the best out of it. One, where all efforts, have come to naught. A marriage where like my mama-in-law only death can give you release. Then I beg you to start talking to those little princesses all around you. Educate them on the effects of whatever decisions they take. Girls should learn to ask men their visions and see if they fit into it before accepting marriage proposals. Understanding your fiancés dreams and plans for the future is perhaps even more important that asking how deep is his love for you.

Women should be taught to speak up and stop being martyrs. Your life should serve as an example. Good or bad!

Many would insult and criticize my mother-in-law but you know what? She's made her mistake and nature and God made things work in her favor. Like I said earlier, a wise person learns from the mistakes of others, we can't experience all ourselves

John Mason said it rightly; "from one I may learn what not to do, while from another, I learn what to do. Learn from the mistakes of others. You can never live long enough to make all the mistakes yourself. You can learn more from a wise man when he is wrong than a fool when he is right"

We as women should care for ourselves too. We owe ourselves the same care and considerations we give to others. Don't be scared to put yourself first when it's right.

Life is for the Living

A word is enough.....

BANKE.

STORY 4

Onome's Story

"Mummy, it's going to be okay!" – My eldest daughter said softly, hugging me tight.

This was becoming a routine that plays out daily, sometimes twice daily during the weekends.

My heart is also broken. The pain unbearable, the loneliness is daunting. Physically, down below-my veejayjay; I am soared all over.

How did life turn around so quickly? How can this be possible? I can hardly believe that less than fifteen months ago, my life was perfect.

I had the love of my life with me; the father to my kids-my home was the envy of all my friends and relatives. Every one kept complementing on how lucky we both were. We were soul mates, we were first loves, companions, best friends, brother/sister, and lovers. Ome was my EVERYTHING.

Yes, everything! In Ome, God packaged my everything. He complements me in every way. He was my mentor, my biggest fan.

Ome! Ome!! Ome!!! Tears continued flowing.

I have cried every day, since the death of my hubby. With me, theories have failed. They say time heals every wound, but the past fifteen months has soaked up in misery, the past twenty years of my life.

The pain, the loneliness- I just want to die, if not for my children. Death is the only solution to this agony. How can one so good, so caring be cut short in his prime. While vagabonds still have life in them.

How do I tell my tale? How do I narrate the torture and pain I pass through daily because of tradition! Tradition!! Hmmm!! Native laws and customs. I can't see beyond tomorrow. I can't see the future… if not for my kids-death is all I wish for.

Before I go into the description of the hell I go through on a daily basis, let me calm myself down by going through memory lane.

I am thirty five years today. Had Ome been here! He always manages to cook up a surprise- every single time. And all the times were all so special.

"My Queen Onome" I can still hear Ome call me. We share same names: both traditional and English- Onome and Hilary, that's how predestined we were. We have same names on everything. All our documents are same, save for my maiden name before his surname.

We were born a day apart; I came first. Our paths crossed again when we were five. Our parents moved into same street, they quickly struck a close relationship, after our mothers recognized each other from their antenatal classes. From our mother's calculations, I came few minutes to midnight while Ome came into this now so terrible world a few hours after midnight, three am to be precise. So we were about three hours separated by birth but were born on two different consecutive days. Our mothers said they both comforted each other throughout the torturous labor pains. They bonded immediately and shared everything together, we shared same matron, bathing soap, baby cosmetics and all. They were parted few days after delivery, but delighted to meet again after five years. Both our parents never conceived after us. We were both only kids. So we bonded deeply.

We spent all the time together, courtesy of our mothers very close friendship. They were like sisters, we went everywhere together, had same toys, matching cloths, same bicycle. We attended same nursery, primary and secondary schools. Not one to blow my own trumpet, I blossomed into quiet a beauty. Ome was also quiet a charmer. Tall, fair-skinned like his half cast mother. And he had gap tooth and dimples. I pinched myself all the time, wondering how lucky I was. To top it all, he was intelligent, caring and generous. Not surprised, he chose to study medicine. He was a very caring doctor-my sexy doctor.

I on the one hand, read Mass Communication, but since we desired to have a large family, we decided that I should be a stay at home mum while he worked. His salary was more than enough to provide for us, give us the luxury we desired and save for the future. We were smart enough to have a separate account for each child that will aid their education.

We had five kids, the last a set of twins. Three girls and two boys, our family was complete, we were fulfilled, and I was overjoyed.

I have always had everything I desired. For a longtime, I had wondered how life has been so generous to me. Loving parents, good body, perfect health, great friends, affectionate and loving hubby. A dedicated father to our kids, gorgeous angelic looking kids and very intelligent children. My own home, choice cars – I get a brand-new car every other year plus vacations to foreign countries. Life was good! I NEVER lacked or longed for anything. I had the best of everything. I had no idea what average meant.

All was going smoothly until that black Tuesday! The day my world ended. The day Ome... passed on! Going back to that day-Hurts!!!! Going over the last time I saw him alive, the last hug, the last kiss awakens the sadness buried within me. On that fateful day, He got home, walked into the kitchen, gave me a hug from behind, sexily rubbing my bum on him and he gave me a wet kiss on my neck. I giggled happily because I knew we had a steamy night ahead-I live for those nights. Ome was the best Lover, though I never had any other, I knew I had one of the best. He picked up his bags and realized he forgot the new swimming costume he got for the kids.

He rushed out to go get them. My plea for him to get it in the morning fell on deaf ears. As he drove out our twins began crying simultaneously. Goose pimples were all over me. I started shaking, my heart beating fast. I ran for my phone in the sitting room and began calling him. I kept calling till someone answered me and told me the owner of the phone had been in a ghastly motor accident and he was in a bad shape. Everything was a blur from then... I had no idea how I got to the hospital, held Ome in my arms and kept kissing him, crying and begging God to intervene. He opened his eyes, took a painful look at me-like he knew something I didn't. He tried to smile, called me my pet name, told me to promise to take good care of our kids no matter what and he asked me not to mourn him but celebrate him because he regrets nothing. That he loved me ONLY and will always do... he died in my arms. It took lots of arms to get me away from him.

Six weeks after, Ome's mum, died in her sleep. It was another fatal blow life dealt me. The dad had passed on seven years earlier. I knew Ome had some cousins and uncles here and there but I was not close to them. He was a busy doctor, while I tended to our kids. Never in my life was I prepared for what laid ahead.

Months after Ome's burial, I was summoned by Ome's extended family. I was told that according to customs & traditions I am still their wife. And now that Ome has passed on to glory, it is customary for me to be given to the next person in line as a wife.

I was like "whaaaaaaattttt!!!!!!!!!!??????"

But that was just me flexing my facial muscle.

To this people, ignorance was not an excuse. I am not even allowed to speak. Whatever decision was taken, I was to comply without hesitating.

Long story short... it was decided that an older cousin of Ome be my new husband. Let me make it clear.

I am now to be a wife to a member of Ome's family, as custom dictates. If Ome had a son from another woman. The son would inherit me. In the absence of this, the next best suited person would take over.

In this case, it happened to be his elder cousin.

The clause was that the cousin may decide to accept me as his wife. But give me free reign over my body. I would then be free to date but not allowed to remarry. He would feed and care for all the needs of my kids and I. but if along the line I decide I can't be lonely any longer and decide to get married, my dowry will be returned. In the case where my decision is to disregard their law to marry their family member, the dowry paid on me, will also be refunded to them. If the man who I was shared /allocated to were to accept me and needs me for his wife, the wife/wives he has at home has no say in the matter. They only have to welcome me as their mate who will now be sharing their husband's bed. In the case where the man accepts and I refused, it would be clear to them that the marriage is over. The dowry would be returned to them. Now the downside to all of this is, any decision or act of mine that leads to my dowry been returned spells only one thing; I lose every right to my children. It means my business with their family is over. They would sever all ties with me and my kids collected. End of discussion.

Of course, I couldn't let that happen.

Today, I am the third wife, to a fifty three years old furniture maker, who drinks local wine, twenty four hours, and seven days a week. He stinks, has a pot belly and is so overweight and there's not a single white teeth in his mouth.

He didn't allow them finish speaking before he agreed to take me in as a wife. Who would blame him? A good looking thirty five years old lady, eighteen years his junior. I am convinced that am the best thing that has happened to him. If not for this terrible arrangement, till his death, there's no way he could have been able to cross my path not to talk about cross my thighs.

We were advised to remain in our mansion, while he my new husband visits us and stays briefly if he likes. But he was told he shouldn't reside there. My husband did not leave a will but all my husband's properties where left the way they are. No one touched it. Not a single thing was confiscated. They didn't even ask me about his properties. I was told by everyone how lucky I was. Some greedy relatives will see reason to put their fingers in Omes hard earned fortune. But I am sure they are nice to me because I am also from their community, I could be their own daughter. I don't think a lady from another part of the country will be treated with such loose hands. So I saw I had one reason to be grateful. But in the case that I had decided to return their dowry, all my husband's properties will be given to the guardian of the kids to manage for them until they are old enough to care for them themselves.

My home was still my home. It's been sixty three days since he started sleeping with me… the first forty five days, (menstrual period and all*sobbing*) he slept with me three times daily without fail; in the wee hours of the morning, during lunch and then at night. He was in my bed daily. All my talks to him about neglecting the other wives fell on deaf ears. At first I thought maybe it's the excitement in sleeping in a tastily furnished house. My bedroom is elegantly decorated, my beddings cost quit a fortune. Sleeping on them is very comfortable. I soon realized it wasn't the bed or the house, I guess I turn him on.

As I speak, I am dead within… I am tempted to call for a family meeting, this is too much. What Ome never attempted to do with my body, this guy is just misusing. I feel violated! The way he ravages me! He savors every minute, grunting in ecstasy. Every single time he is on me, disbelieve and shock ripple through my whole body, I always shed tears...but he is deaf to that. Fate has dealt him a good deal and he is making the best of it. I am sure he would be the envy of all the men in our community. All through the act, I keep asking myself; how did I get here? This dirty pig, unshaved with hairs all over, after sticking it into dirty, un-kept women, he comes here to me without even a condom.

I still have his smell stuck in my nostrils hours after he has gone. No matter the shower gel or body spray, I can't get his stinking odor off of me. I don't think he knows what shaving is all about. There's hair everywhere! It's a psychological, physical and emotional battle. Nothing but pure Torture! How is this possible? How?

I never knew that my glamorous traditional native laws and custom marriage was me been traded into something I had never imagined. So there's another thing tied to dowry been paid? Marriage is to the family not the individuals? How was I to know that this would happen? If I had no children it would have been a done deal but how do I leave five children that has been brought up solely by me with the best of care to someone else with less credibility. It's not something to even contemplate!

"Mum! Mum!!! We want to eat burger" my third daughter Cassandra screamed.

"No! We want pancakes!!......" the twins screamed to counter her.

"Okay, okay...everyone will get what they want. Just give me one minute sweets!" I replied, as I stood up... still sore from the violent so called mid-day copulation from my new husband. I could barely move properly. His love making has gotten longer I noticed, probably taking some local herbs to give him better erection and enough strength. I proceeded downstairs.

As I walked into my kitchen; I saw foodstuffs everywhere. He bought more foodstuffs again?! Did I just smile? I looked around. My kitchen and pantry are filled beyond its capacity. He was asked to care for us and I won't lie, he's doing his job perfectly. He has exceeded my expectations. I wonder where he gets the cash from. Can furniture making be so profitable? There's no food that's not in my pantry- both Local and Foreign. Every item he buys-Double, some triple. I have galloons of everything. Everything is in excess. He has of recent proceeded to the kids needs. He took them shopping and I tagged along just to see how it goes. Silently eager to see him baffled at the expensive taste they have. And gloat as he checks from one pocket to another wondering how he would pay the huge bill. Girl! Was I disappointed! The twins had their own trolley, the others a single one to themselves. And they shopped to their hearts content. He paid for items a little over two hundred thousand naira without batting an eyelid. I realized he did that to know their tastes. From then on; their expensive breakfast cereals, their juices, chocolates and all that they use he buys in cartons. He takes them swimming, to the cinema and for drive out. From the beginning of this arrangement till date, I have not gone to the bank, to make any withdrawals, instead I send my girls to go make deposits.

As I went about, preparing the burger and pancakes. I wondered how long I could keep up with this-the sexual aspect and the effects of having a strange man in my bed, I mean. My parents are scared to offend our ancestors by aiding me in anyway. They fear to lose their only child to death. The ancestors/forefathers they say... are merciless.

Friends have all deserted me. They probably think I am done for. They see this as the end of me. That my relevance to society has been affected negatively with this turn of events. But I know better. Their conclusion on my matter is not my headache. It doesn't bother me one bit.

My main concern is my physical, emotional and psychological health. If I don't do something fast, I will die from a combination of different ailments. And with five kids-I have a full twenty four hours schedule.

Burgers, potato pancakes and freshly made water melon juice were grasped hungrily as they positioned in front of the TV. My God! What beautiful kids... how do I handle this?

I can't take any rash decisions. I am the only child of both living parents, from the same tribe as Ome. If I run away with my children and loose a parent in my absence who will bury them? The shame and stigma on the family name would be a burden on my family. Can I be selfish? Is there no way around this? I do not intend to marry again, Never! God, how can I do right by Ome?

Running away would cause a rift between my kids and their ancestral lineage. They would forever be seen as cast out and never welcomed with open arms for anything. Yes, I could remain in Diaspora. But what if my daughters in a twist of fate, happen to fall in love with Nigerian men who insist on getting married traditionally at Omes family compound? What stories will they and their suitors be greeted with? If my daughters were to marry from our place, would it not affect their relationships? Won't I be seen as a disrespect of law and customs? Will my decision now not affect them later?

What about my sons, if one of them were to hold a political position? Would their people accept him after I might have taken a rash decision and fled with them? They would always be tension and things and issues will never go swiftly for them.

Diplomacy… thorough brainstorming is all I need!

"Ring… ring…!" my phone beeps, I answered! It's my new husband calling to ask if I will love to eat suya (barbequed meat) I told him yes. Whenever he buys suya… I can't place the value in naira because we are never able to finish it. All six of us-including the helps. We always have left over for the next day.

This man is eager to please me. An Idea clicked in my head. Now that I still intoxicate him, may be I should try something.

I rushed to the kitchen. Cooking up a new plan in mind-I got to work!

Hours later, he is here. I personally opened the door for him and invited him in. kids where in their private parlor upstairs where I had instructed the helps not to let them out and send them to bed at the appropriate time. I won't be seeing them till tomorrow. I have their future in my hands and I have to make sure everything went fine for them.

I took my new husband by hand and led him up the stairs to my bedroom. I made sure I bent down a few times to give him a glimpse of what was hidden beneath. I caught him licking his lips with bulging eyes. Sexy cool blues playing on my inbuilt home theater. Once there, I took off my very sexy housecoat, to reveal nothing but a very sexy Red bra with matching G-string. He almost passed out. I slowly undressed him and I took him with me into my bathroom where my Jacuzzi was set with steaming fragrance filled bubble bath. I deliberately used musk because the fragrance makes me go wild! There I ushered him in and slowly scrubbed him squeaky clean. I took the opportunity to brush his mouth too.

We proceeded to the bedroom, where I had a table set for two- with candles, a beautifully set centerpiece, well laid out cutleries and dishes. I prepared one of our native delicacies he had said in passing was his favorite. I feed him a very delicious meal. Yes, fed… with my own hands! Then we proceeded to the bed. I teased him a bit and did a short strip tease like I use to do for Ome. Our bedroom moments were always fun, fun, fun. I tried to focus on the Project on ground. When I noticed that he couldn't take anymore, I joined him in Bed-where we had desert. I was a specialist in making dessert, having five kids had made me an expert. I fed him his portion of ice-cream and even gave him some from my own mouth and licked mine off different choice part of his body. I first took a large scoop and placed it on one of his nipples. He screamed at the coldness and was delighted to have my warm tongue lick it off of him. By the time I proceeded to other parts-My new hubby was screaming profanities, as my tongue began working wonders in places I guess he never knew existed. He tried to hold me but I didn't let him lift a finger. Ice-cream finished, I went down below with ice cubes in my mouth. He was very ready and when I took him in my mouth, the feeling of the ice cubes and my tongue made him scream for mercy. I paid him no mind and went on rocking his world, believe it or not, by this stage this man was shedding tears amidst his moans. I began to wonder silently... has he never been given a blow job. I know I am very good at it, but this tears? All the better anyway. I continued not stopping for even a second. I guess the drugs he took made him last so very long.

When he couldn't hold himself anymore, I jumped on him and rode him mercilessly...he was moaning uncontrollably, holding on to my hips for dear life. He filled every part of me and he was still very hard, as I navigated my hips to different angles, I couldn't help but feel cold shrills run down my spine, every hair on my body standing. I don't know if he sensed I was aroused but before I knew it, he threw me off him and stood up. Without wasting a second he lifted me up and began feasting on my boobs. That was my weakest link. The next few minutes or was it hours, saw me having a taste of my own medicine. I couldn't hold up all the pent up feelings, my body betrayed me and I could hear myself scream in delight, this minute he was behind, the next he is beside me, the next he is on top, I managed to hold him down once more as I climbed on him and rode hard, before long I found myself having an orgasm... I was shocked!! It's been months since Ome died and despite having the urge often, I have never given any consideration to it. All the times new husband was on me, I have never been there fully with him so I never get to climax. Today was different. I usually rest after an orgasm with Ome but this dude wouldn't let me rest a second, he continued like nothing happened and I was sure I will die from it all but I was shocked to find myself having another orgasm. How is this possible?

While relaxing... I noticed tears in his eyes. I pretended not to see. He asked me what I wanted... Smart man! I kept quiet and resumed working on him, when I noticed he was hard again. He refused to go home that night. Which was perfect, because I had more tricks up my sleeves. And because of the local herbs he takes, he was soon up and ready to go. We both had a satisfactory night...I am ashamed to admit it. With Ome it was slow and gentle, but here I was experiencing something I could not explain.

I tried not to feel guilty. But it was impossible. Here I am on our bed, with another man. Not been taken advantage of this time but having mega fun even though that was not the plan. I made note to get a 10years family planning solution FAST!

Six months later...

Life has been less traumatic... I have decided to fight and not be a victim. Just like Robert Schuller puts it-'Tough time's never last-but tough people do'

As I speak, my kids and I are at the airport... checking in! We are relocating to the States. I managed to convince Ono (new hubby-I call him by name now. He has earned it) that I needed a change of environment. I also made him realize that he also needs to broaden his horizons... with our real estate properties in the US and all my kids been citizens I was given an extended visa. Am going to be a full time nanny, till the kids are grown. I got good private schools for the kids and they cost quite a fortune. But we have good source of income to cover all bases. We are well financially... and Ono takes his responsibility hundred percent well.

Ono is tagging along. It's his first trip to the United States. Prior to this trip, I have coerced him to go with me to Dubai, South Africa and Cape Verde-He footed the bill. He no longer wears that local attitude and spending loads of time with the kids and I has affected him positively. The way he speaks, the television programs he watches, the kind of food he eats-All changed. And he has lost impressive weight. He looks smart now. I take very good care of him and everyone has been applauding us. I never get to know how he operates with his other families but a timetable was set and he sticks to it. We see him on days we are scheduled to have him. His business has taken a positive turn as he has opened more branches around the country. With a little financial assistance from me of course.

He got a two year visiting visa to the U.S and will spend the first one month with us. After then he will visit every three months and spend twenty-eight days with us on each visit.

My family is happy, and Ome's family is the happiest! I am at peace. My kids are at peace. They love Ono so much. I have also grown very fond of him.

I do not agree with this part of our tradition and I personally think the whole thing is absurd. But when faced with it, I found a way out. Using my brains helped me out. Having loads of money at my disposal also played a role in placing things in order.

Some women whose hubby is not well to do may have it difficult. They may have to forfeit their rented apartment to move into the new hubby's apartment. And living with another family is not an easy issue. The widow and her kids would forever be treated badly by the original wife and the children. In my case, Ono's business was very profitable and he was making loads of money. He has started to import furniture's too.

He is not the lazy type and very good at his job. With Ome's contacts he had more contracts than he could handle. Many women are given to men who are lazy. Men that can't even fend for their own family, not to even speak of the poor widow given to him. There are so many factors that makes this decision a hell for women who fall into it.

I now see that I was favored. I have grown to be fond of Ono as I stated earlier and we relate very well. I am sexually satisfied-One hundred and ten percent fulfilled. I would never have guessed that this would happen. Other unlucky women may have the reverse as the case. Where they are daily raped by men who are now their husbands. They are left to live a life of sexual frustration whereas their late hubby's had given them total fulfillment.

Some are never again made to feel special. The lifestyle they are used to is cut off. The kids are affected in every way and where the woman has no source of income, one can only pray for them because their plight can only be imagined.

So many others are not so lucky. And daily they are dealt with badly. But with our unshakable culture…our very stiff traditions… what can a woman do? We are tied down. I chose in my situation to wake up and fight to be alive for my kids, instead of dying of misery. It was a difficult decision but it was between having my kids been brought up by a total stranger, risking their inheritance with a stranger or sticking to traditions. You all know my decision.

My kid's come first…and I know you agree with me.

Onome

STORY 5

Adeni's Story

50 WOMEN WHO CHANGED THE WORLD

Inspirational and influential female pioneers.

"Whatever their chosen field – from politics and pop stardom to fashion and feminism – women have been leaving their mark on the world since time began. In celebration of these inspiring trailblazers and to mark the one hundred and second international women's day today (Friday, eight March) – we've selected our top females who have affected life as we know in their personal way…

By Anna Pollitt
Stylist.co.uk......

I looked further down the screen of my laptop and continue reading…

1. **Millicent Fawcett** – "A large part of the present anxiety to improve the education of girls and women is also due to the

conviction that the political disabilities of women will not be maintained…"

I looked further and read on… Fawcett dedicated her life to the peaceful fight for women's rights.

2. **Colo Chanel** – "Fashion fades, only style remains the same." The daughter of a laundry woman and a market stall holder, she worked as a club singer and hat maker before becoming one of the greatest fashion designers the world has ever seen.

3. **Queen Elizabeth I** – "I have already joined myself in marriage to a husband namely the kingdom of England."

The formidable daughter of Henry VIII, Elizabeth oversaw the defeat of the Spanish Armada during one of the most successful reigns in England's history

4. **Marie Curie** – "Noting in life is to be feared. It is only to be understood." Best known for her work on radioactivity, the Polish-French physicist and chemist was the first person to receive two Nobel prizes, the first female professor at the university of Paris and the first woman to be enshrined in Frances National Mausoleum, the Paris Pathelon, on her own merits.

"Can you beat that…? I said to myself and went on reading.

5. **Diana, Princess of Wales** – "Everyone needs to be valued. Everyone has the potential to give something back."

6. **Boudicca** – "If you weigh well the strengths of our armies, you will see that in this battle we must conquer or die. This is a woman's resolve. As for the men, they may live or be slaves."

The British warrior Queen led an unprecedented and bloody revolt against the occupying Roman Empire in 61 AD, making her an important cultural icon.

7. **Benazir Bhutto** – "Democracy is the best revenge."

As the 11th prime minister of Pakistan, Bhutton was the first woman to head a Muslim state. She ended military dictatorship in the country, and was noted for her battle for women's rights. She was assassinated in a suicide attack in 2007.

"Waooh!!! A Muslim woman did this? Shocking….. This is nothing but pure courage.

8. **Mary Wollstone Craft** – "It is vain to expect virtue from women till they are in some degree independent of men."

   Described as the Mother of feminism, the 18th century British writer was best known for her most important work. (A vindication of the Rights of the Woman) She was the mother of writer **Mary Shelley**, who would find fame as an author too for her novel "Frankenstein."

   "So a woman wrote "Frankenstein?".... That's impressive"... I thought to myself. "Are there no African women on this impressive list?" I may need to scroll down. These women have all really changed the world in their own ways...

   "Oh! Madonna.... I got to read this"...

Madonna – "I'm tough, I'm ambitious, and I know exactly what I want, if that makes me a bitch, okay."

The imitable and constantly evolving singer has sold more than 300 million records, as well as turning her hand to songwriting, acting, film-directing and producing, fashion designing and writing children's books"

"One woman... multi-talented!!!.... Where are the Africans... hey!!?" I kept scrolling down and came to Oprah!! Yeah!" I smiled and went on it read.

Oprah Winfrey – "Be thankful for what you have, you'll end up having more. If you concentrate on what you don't have, you will never, ever have enough"

Born to a poor single mother in Mississippi, the phenomenally successful US talk show host and media proprietor is reportedly worth $ 2.7 billion and is a generous philanthropist...

"Hmmm.... Wonderful... a woman born to a poor single mother... later I am going to take out some alone time and read her Biography through and through"

Hilary Clinton – "In too many instances, the march to globalization has also meant the marginalization of women and girls. And that must change"

Helena Rubinstein – "Hard work keeps the wrinkles out of the mind and spirit."

The polish-born make-up entrepreneur immigrated to Australia in 1902 without money or the ability to speak English. She went on to create one of the world's first cosmetics companies after mixing Lanolin the grease found in merino Sheep wool with Scented flowers – making one of the world's richest women in the process.

Margaret Thatcher – "If you set out to be liked, you would be prepared to compromise on anything at any time, and you would achieve nothing."

Mother Theresa "Not all of us can do great things. But we can do small things with great love!"

Nancy Wake – "I was too busy to be afraid"

Angela Merkel – "Nobody in Europe will be abandoned. Nobody in Europe will be excluded. Europe only succeeds if we work together."

The first female Chancellor of Germany, Angela Merkel Presides over the largest and most powerful European economy and what is considered to be the world most powerful economy in the world after the US and Japan.

"Can you beat that...?"

Virginia Woolf – "For most of history…. Anonymous was a woman"

Aung Sang Sun kyi – "In societies whose men are truly confident of their own worth, women are not merely tolerated but valued.

Condoleezza Rice

The former US Secretary of State voted the most powerful woman in the world by Forbes in 2004 and 2005 drew both praise and criticism during her time as George W.

Bush's right hand woman. A talented musician, she originally set out to be a concert pianist.

Michelle Obama – "There are still many causes worth sacrificing for, so much history yet to be made."

Why can't I get something about pure black African Women? I wondered. I continued my search on Google till I came to Forbes 20 youngest Power women in Africa....ten minutes later page not opening. Too much hassles opening the site, I came across a contributor, a blogger 'Mfonobong Nsehe', who did a compilation of same twenty powerful women in African and I settled down to read....

"All the twenty (20) women are all under the age of forty-five (45) who has wielded enormous influence in African business, technology, policy and media"... it read. Among them are

- Ory Okolloh Kenyan, founder Ushahidi
- Chimamanda Adichie, Nigerian Writer
- Yolanda Cuba South African, Corporate Executive
- Ndidi Nwuneli, Nigerian Social Entrepreneur
- Dambisa Moyo, Zambian Economist
- Khanyi Ndhlomo, South African Media Mogul
- Phuti Melabie, South African, Shanduka Group
- Funmi Iyanda, Nigerian, Journalist & Broadcaster
- Isis Nyongo, Kenyan, Managing Director, Africa
- Bethlehem Tilahum Alemu, Ethiopian Entrepreneur
- Elsie Kanza Tanzania, Advisor to Tanzania's president.
- Julie Gichuru Kenyan, Journalist & Broadcaster
- Lisa Kropman, South African, Entrepreneur
- Stella Kilonzo, Kenyan. Chief Executive, Capital Markets Authority, Kenya.
- Magatte Wade, Senegalese
- Jonitha Gugu Mgibi, South African Senior Partner, Ernst & Young.
- June Arunga Kenya Entrepreneur.
- Olga Kimani–Arara. Kenyan. Google country manager, Kenya.
- Saran Kaba Jones, Liberian Founder Face Africa

"Hmm…." Quite a list …. I see my daughters name on such a list someday….

"Mum!!" Nicole Screamed from outside… "Am in here baby!"… I responded.

All this while, I have been hooked unto another world. A world where women made a difference. A world where the girl child actually had significance.

Nicole is my last child… She is six, far smarter than her age. From the first few weeks of her life, I realized she was special. 'An old soul'. She's very chubby, some might regard her as obese. The truth is that she has always been big. She weighed a massive 8.8kg at twelve weeks and has kept adding. She has long black hair, cute round face, dimples and dark chocolate skin. And a very sharp tongue. She is also very flexible despite her weight. She is always running about, never walking. I still can't understand why she can't slow down. It's like she is in a rush to get everything done and grow old. Whenever she is excited she jumps on her toes.

"Mum!!"… She ran in, panting "I need you to read me that story now!! Like right noooowww!!! Thank you, very much!!…"

"My small dictator…" I said smiling. She always gave orders. She makes it known with every opportunity given that she's the baby of the house and that her desires and needs ought to be respected and placed first above others.

Nicole looked at me for affirmation. Immediately I said yes! She flew to her room and returned with a collection of Disney stories. I knew she would ask for Snow white. She never gets tired of me reading that. And after reading to her, she bombards me with endless questions. Why this? Why not that? I have told her to write her own Snow white story; the way she thinks it would be nice. And who knows someone might make it into a movie!

She told me, she would think about it and tell me her decision later.

Hours later. All kids bathed and tucked in. I was left alone to my thoughts.

I couldn't remember the last time; I enjoyed the companion of my hubby. Just to spend time together. Talk about stuff. It's been three weeks since I last saw him. He sneaks in and out. I hear the sound of his car coming in and leaving. But I never get to see him. Yes it's possible. We live in a two winged mansion.

After having six girls, He has long concluded that I was worthless! My luck ran out when I had Nicole Six years ago. He made it clear that I was a regrettable disappointment.

I on the one hand, have long accepted my destiny or fate or whatever. There's nothing I haven't tried to make peace in my matrimonial home and make him see reasons. All I tried, bore no tangible results. He sees his daughters and he cringes (*sobs*).

But it's okay. I had earlier in the day done a lot of reading and I am reassured that my six Divas are no mistakes. No way!! Irrespective of what culture or tradition dictates right now. I will do my best.

I will make sure I stay alive be healthy role models for my kids. Be there for them all through the way. Enjoying the rides of their lives as they pursue their dreams and be there to lend a shoulder when tides are down. And also be there to rejoice with them when things are great.

I definitely will be my best at each of their weddings... Hmmmm.... Weddings!!

I sure have a great role to play and it starts now. Despite my loneliness, I have come to realize it has some advantages; no man around the house, throwing tantrums, been possessive, monitoring my every move-none of that. Right now I am a 'single' married woman. My kids get the best financially, that alone is heart soothing. I will save and plan their lives wisely. Save for good schools, pursue foreign scholarship, who knows we may relocate outside Nigeria for a while to give them a foreign exposure-a change in culture. I know dear hubby will be more than glad to have us off his radar.

God knows I have got my work cut out for me.

Kris Jenner!! She came to mind and I find myself smiling. I could be like her-the Nigerian version of her...*winks*. Later in life, I could manage my kids. Anything is possible.

I won't lie about lonely nights but what can I do? In order to be a role model to my daughters; I have to keep a loyal profile. I won't cheat. I have alternatives no matter how less satisfying it may seem. It's better than nothing. I have been experimenting with playing with myself and its nerves cooling. I have to be satisfied with that.

Now that my path has been defined I feel a sense of calm, peace. I may not have been where I thought I should be in life. But I know a lot of adventure awaits me.

"Deep breath"

I have for long stopped to wonder why female children are seen as inferior in this part of the world. Watching a series on the channel 'Telemundo'; I have also realized that Indians do the same. Now I am indifferent.

I wake up daily to the giggles and playful batters of my six daughters. Different exciting personalities brooding. Each daughter has her unique trait and beauty. And what beauties they are. As I speak, I am getting emotional. I began childbearing very early, thank God for that, because for the past fifteen years, I have not known rest.

First came – Zara (fourteen)

Then Vida (twelve)

Followed by Petra (ten),

The twins Ariana & Alicia (eight) and her royal Majesty-Nicole (six)

Haaaa!!! I am one exhausted mother. But I won't trade the fun for anything. Everything is perfect. From the morning chatters, as they bath and get dressed (all so very orderly and neat) to the breakfast table is loads of fun. They all have so much to say to each other. It is like a girl's hostel. I have four live-in helps that are all female too and also a cook. We are all twelve in number. The drive to school is a movie in itself. Their loud chatter. One can only imagine.

On Sunday's on our trip to church and out for our weekly fun time together is so much fun. I won't trade my life for another. The gist always flows. The fun is mad fun. Whenever we go out shopping; I am always the cynosure of all eyes. Every one stares at me with my six beautiful daughters. All dressed to the T. Having one beautiful daughter fills your heart with so much pride, now multiply that by six!! My heart is bursting at its seams.

Their academic work is examplenary. They participate well in children and teens church. I am yet to confront a problem. Asides from my second daughter Vida, who wants to be a rock star –There are no very serious issues yet.

I am also faced with picky eating from the older ones. I am naturally a slim person. At forty-four, I am a comfortable size ten. So all my daughters save for the last one is chubby, the other all have my slim silhouette.

My hubby has not had sexual relations with me for six years. It's been six years of long lonely nights but I have got a full house. And I have no time to be sad. I am too preoccupied with raising my precious damsels.

I am also plagued with the stigma of having female children and no male issue. But I have decided to rise above my challenge. I have had six girls. That's my limit. My life is set.

Or so I thought!

I was summoned by my in-laws, all of whom I have a good relationship with. In Nigeria, it's funny how your in-laws have 'ALL' the final say. They are 'ALWAYS' Right and can do no wrong. They are like semi-god and that's because whatever they say or decide 'Stands'. Here in my beloved country a 'WIFE' has no say, inside her home with her hubby-she can speak, but when in the midst of her hubbys family no matter the degrees she has, she expected to be quiet. She is not entitled to any opinion and it's a taboo to even voice it if she's bold to abhor one.

That particular Sunday, I dressed up gorgeously. I always made an effort to look dab when I go out. Am still in pretty good shape. I was asked to present 'ONLY' myself. That is to mean, I shouldn't come with any of my family members. I had no issues with any of them, so I was confident that whatever the meeting was about, they would definitely put me into due consideration, that I was very confident of. I am truly blessed to have great in-laws. So I arrived their family compound gracefully with a clear conscience.

I met them all seated, having drinks like there was a small party been held before my arrival. I remember seeing my hubby's car parked well into the compound signifying that he has been here quite a while. But I didn't see him when I walked in.

I tried to do a mental calculation as to the time I actually last laid eyes on him... was it five or six days ago? He stopped sleeping home since way back when and I stopped counting Jare' (Local Nigerian slang, connoting; non-chalance) I also noticed there where only elders in the meeting, no youngsters like me (Laughing; I am a youngster please!)

I sat down gracefully, I felt good, Smelt good, tasted good (yea, tasted!!) and looked GLAM. Confidence oozing. I looked classy, am classy! Well read, soft spoken, pretty face, glowing skin and a superb figure. I was all smiles, because God knows that from the bottom of my heart, I was truly happy. I am alive.... Yeah!! Six daughters woke up this Sunday morning, all body organs functioning-mentally and psychological okay. I can't ask for anything else. I can't.

I noticed that my composure made the other members of my family quite uncomfortable. The women, especially. Why is big Aunty so pale? And small aunty keeps shifting from one position to the other on that small sofa, she's sitting on. Why the sad faces?

I have been through hell. And back. I have mastered the act of smiling and looking composed no matter the battles going on inside of me. I couldn't show how heart broken I used to feel when my hubby treated me ill when we first got married. My daughters watched me keenly. So I couldn't dare be sad. I had my own private time, I sit, soliloquize and cry if need be, and then I get up, dust myself off and face the rest of the day. It's always buried between two- three am at night.

If these guys think they are about to throw me a bomb shell... Eish! Then they are so completely ignorant of the phrase 'what does not kill you – makes you strong!!' That phrase!! Hey!! It's so true neh?!!"

Someone cleared their throat, signifying that they are about to begin. Every one sat quietly and watched. My hubby appeared from an inner room and sat down calmly. He made a conscious effort to avoid my gaze. We didn't try to pretend to be civil. We openly ignored each other. I did not bother to throw a greeting his way. My Family-I call them that, because I have grown to love them very deeply. They welcomed me and accepted me with open arms and never made me feel sad or unhappy. I ran him down silently and found I was stimulated sexually. Hmmm, still hot as ever! I missed having Him in my bed. Eish! We had so many HOT!! HOT!! HOT!! HOTTER THAN FIRE bedroom memories, Humph! I breathed heavily and fanned myself with my beautiful crafted hand fan – I came prepared. I looked around the room, I was so sure everyone could read my lustful thoughts. I had goose pimples all over me. I calmed myself and focused on the matter on ground.

The eldest man on my hubby's paternal side began speaking on marriage in West Africa and Nigeria in particular. He spoke extensively on polygamy and condemned the westernization of every thing in Nigeria. He said in the olden days, men marry four to six wives and they all lived in harmony.

He then narrowed his talk to the importance of male children in family. He talked much, trying to make me see reason with them to the best of his capabilities. I wonder why he worried. By the time I had my third girl, I had been schooled by everyone from hubby himself to neighbors to Church members to even cab drivers. I am well educated on that matter. I have a PhD on it. There's nothing new he can add to it. I sat down calmly, pretending to be taking in all the bullcrap he was spitting out – I glared quickly round the room, scared that my thoughts may have been heard.

Then he hit the nail on the head. My hubby is taking a second wife, who is pregnant with a son. The ultrasound scan confirmed it.

"Wow!!!" ... I was all smiles. See, sincerely speaking I am happy. I loved my hubby. Now I love him less by the day, but I still love him. I am still sexually attracted to him. He is the father of the six beautiful damsels I bore and most importantly He 'cares' for us. He provides everything.

We all use the latest gadgets. My daughters have all the trendy fashion gadgets. If we all put down our iphones and ipads and other small you know... the value of the items can buy a good Honda Accord

2007 Sedan Car. Now you get the picture! Am going to be a witch, if I can hate on him and wish him bad. He desires a male son and I couldn't give him that. And I see how saddened and depressed He had been for not having a son to play with. He needs someone to take over from him and bear his name. This is Africa and he is acting African. He feels less of a man. He feels deprived and incomplete. I totally get him; I just didn't expect him to dump the kids and me emotionally. He acts like am the cause of this issue. When I reminded him, it's what he deposits in me that determines the sex of the babies he defended himself by saying my womb rejects male children and only opens up to the XX Zygote. *laughing* Pain makes people think illogically.

I know what I mean by been illogical. Haven't you heard a woman looking for the fruit of the womb for years, out of desperation tells God? God please let me just get pregnant, let my belle grow big, when people have seen that I am at least pregnant, let the child go even if it's at seven months, let miscarriage happen, but God let people see me pregnant! Shocking Hey?!

How about a lady of forty-two, who says God let me just get married even if its only two months my marriage will last, let people at least see that I got married. Let me have the experience, wear a white gown and all, let my enemies be put to shame. If the marriage dissolves in two months, I don't care"

Well I got to that plateau also, I think after my fourth daughter, and I saw the pain in my husband's eyes when he held my daughter. I died over and over again. He had nothing to say. But the pain in his eyes was so deep, it engulfed all of him. Right there I would have given any thing to have a son in his arms. His own son. His blood.

When the fifth girl came and then finally the sixth, I was desperate to give him a son. I knew then how Sarah (Biblical Sarah) felt that she had no choice but to ask Abraham to go into her maid. Abraham must have been all moody and depressed, withdrawn and unhappy as my hubby.

For a long time, I had fantasized about my hubby having a male child that I could have welcomed, any idea with opened arms no matter how ridiculous it would have sounded to others. And I'm just emotionally and psychologically drained with all these son, son and son brouhaha-anything to stop it, satisfy dear husband and give me and my girls some peace would be welcomed.

Now after six years of pondering and wondering, the solution finally arrived. And I should not smile? Now my hubby will have a son, my daughters a brother and I shouldn't smile? Was I not aware that I am through with childbirth? Of course I have known that if a son is to come, it can't come from me... So it's all good.

I was still looking at my hubby, He was looking away, he has been avoiding my gaze since he walked in and sat down. He should be happy. I kept my cool. They were also quiet as if waiting for me to say something. I kept on been quiet.

They took my silence to mean that they can move on with the discussion and they were right about that. So they proceeded and gave me the whole low down. Dear hubby has already done the necessary introductory ceremony of the lady to her family and to his. Now what I am getting is that they summoned me here to inform me and do one or two things.

First they asked my stand. I quickly stated that I don't have any problem with another woman coming in as my mate. They thanked me and said that the family does not want their male son to be illegitimate. So the dowry of the pregnant lady will have to be paid. Again I was asked what my stand is. In my head I am like "are these guys for real? I have heard about men marrying without the knowledge of the first wife or not even considering telling the senior wife. She wakes up to see a woman moving into her home.

Again I told them. I have stated sincerely that I have no issues. They thanked me and went ahead to talk about all my amazing years with them as their wife.

Then they told me that they would need me to name anything that my husband will do for me. ANYTHING that will make me happy.

I didn't have to think about that. I thanked them, for all the love they have showered on me and I told them my request was quite simple. That he should be home to see the kids at least three times a week and he should try and be in my bed at least once a week.

They said that is my right and my kids right too. I shouldn't have to demand for it. I simply explained that I didn't mean this as an avenue to air our dirty laundry but dear hubby hasn't touched me for six years!! At that statement everywhere erupted in noisy exclamations. Everyone was talking at once, both his parents, now standing over him.

Everyone was talking. Angry remarks were flying here and there. All eyes looking to me; with sincere pity. Finally, there was silence. The eldest man resumed talking.

He said he could not even put his feelings to words. That at seventy-plus he still tries to satisfy his wife not to mention my hubby. He said he has a daughter my age and would be so pained if any man treats his daughter same.

He said the meeting has to be postponed till ninety days time. In those ninety days, dear hubby will have to return home fully. And back to my bed. No negotiations. After he has bonded himself with the kids and me, only then will the dowry of the other lady be paid.

Someone asked if the baby won't be borne by then... They did some calculations and decided on forty –five days.

The forty-five days, he will have to be home without excuses. After then we will be called and a routine put in place. Both wives had to have conjugal rights. It will also be the duty of the younger wife to cook for our hubby. If I offer food, it's because I want to do it or dear hubby asked for it.

Also, I was asked again to name what I what. I told them that, I will be busy the next ten years. So I would need a source of income before I go back into active business. I would want a business I can do from home. And I need a trust for each daughter.

They asked dear hubby how much he can cough up. He told them ten million naira to be paid in four years. But no trust for our daughters. He said he has an account opened for each of them with regards to their university education. Also, He stated that he has made a very reasonable will. We all agreed that was fair enough.

Having settled all that, they proceeded to invite the lady in... I balanced myself. Ready for the unpredictable, this is Nigeria after all.

I have heard stuff. Cousins have babies for their cousin's hubby. Blood sister's married to one man. House helps becoming second wife, and so on. So it would be difficult to throw me off of my balance.

Then some women left, I watched them return and sat down. Then she walked in. I breathed a sigh of relief. I don't know this pretty young lady from Adam. She is cute. I give her that. Chocolate complexion and chubby.

She couldn't be more than twenty-three. She looks simple, not extravagant. That could be a decoy. But I didn't really care. Seriously!

She was asked to kneel before me and greet me. She did that. Then she stood up. She was given a stool to sit by the door. Then they asked her to tell us about herself.

She said she's from the same village with us. A graduate of Business Education. Just rounded up her youth service. She is the second child, the first daughter of five kids. A Christian.

She was told that her dowry will be paid anytime from two months from when the meeting's held. And she was educated on the rules and regulations of the family. Then she was asked to leave.

They thanked me and told me they hope they have me in their lives as wife forever. That fate has dealt us a blow but the male son is a figure head in Africa and a necessity to ensure future lineage. I thanked them on my knees. I couldn't stand up. They could see the happiness in me. I got in a three hours meeting what I could not battle out on my own these last six years. My kids would see their father more often and my bed would no longer be cold.

They apologized for the abstinence and proceeded to tell him, he needs to be home from this very night.

The driver was asked to take my car home while I join him in his. I don't know how the young lady left but I didn't see her when we came out.

We got into dear hubby's new car and for the first time since he had his security detail, I rode with him. We had armed security driving before and after us. Blaring Sirens all over as we drove. Is this how it felt? Ego somewhere in the inside of me swelled.

Dear hubby instructed the driver to stop by a Chinese restaurant. We stopped. Door opened, we got down. He ushered me into this very exclusive Chinese restaurant and we had dinner. He ordered take out for the kids and all the nannies even the cook.

We didn't talk much, while having dinner. Just monologues about the kid's preferences.

He stopped again at a shopping mall, which was on our way. He sent someone in for Ice cream and pizza. I was surprised that He remembered each of the kid's favorite flavors and pizza toppings.

Then we proceeded to go home. But once again He stopped at a wine shop. And there he did extensive shopping. The bar at home has been for long deserted. And I was sure he had decided to stock it now that he will be home often.

We drove home in silence. The kids would explode with joy when they see their dad. I didn't tell them the news, though my fingers were itchy. Surprising them would be best. And I was right. Even Zara, who I thought would be a bit reserved due to her age and awareness on the issue, flew past me with jet speed into his arms. They hugged him so tight like he would disappear. They were all telling him, how they missed him so much.

They hugged him and refused to let go. I stood by watching, tear's flowing down my cheeks.

He looked up to me and I saw tears running down this face. He mouthed a silent "I'm sorry" shaking his head. I could see he was overwhelmed with emotions as he rested his head on Zara's head. She's quite tall now. He looked at each one of them very surprised to see how beautiful and grown they were. I could see pride in his eyes.

I decided to go in and be a few steps ahead of him, because I anticipated what was coming. Thinking of it made me weak-kneed. I ran in, straight to my room to put everything right. As at this morning I had no idea a man will be in my bed again ever. I had long given up and tried to be focused. I knew I had my vibrator somewhere close. That has to go. Like now!!! I dived for it; arm stretched, picked it and shoved it inside one hand bag I hardly use.

Next, straight to my bathroom. I picked up his favorite foam bath; I lit some candles and undressed while the Jacuzzi gets filled. As I stood naked in the bathroom, the thought of Abiye in my bed, sent cold shivers down my spine. It's been six years, two months and three days, my knees gave way. I held my bathroom door for support and sat on the loo trembling like a teenager.

I could hear the kids screaming and all talking at once. That's the beauty of having live-in nanny's, I have my 'me-time' unperturbed. The nanny's knew the routine; they would bathe and get them ready for bed. I will see them later in bed or tomorrow morning, if I am too busy this night. Dad already bought them dinner and Pizza.

I slipped into the Jacuzzi and closed my eyes. The events of the early evening, very fresh on my mind. My thought went to the pregnant girl- my mate to be and I couldn't sincerely have an opinion about the matter. I just didn't care. Could it be years of silently fighting loneliness, depression, rejection on my own? I had perfected the act of smiling to cover my pains. Even I, had believed my own lies.

Let tomorrow's problems take care of themselves. I tried to calm my self down and focus on the night ahead.

Almost an hour later. I heard Abiye come into my room. I swear I could hear my heart beating about in chaos.

"Adeni? Baby??" Abiye was calling out to me, footsteps approaching. Is this real? Is this me?

"In here…." I replied.

He walked in… came close, knelt down.

And he started apologizing. Tears flowed down my cheeks. I had long concluded on spending the rest of my life alone with my kids. And I honestly do not have an idea on how to go about it. I don't know what to do about this second wife situation but I believe this is Africa. A way must come emerge.

I accepted his apology. It's only in Nigeria; a man can walk out of his matrimonial home and walk back in, expecting the wife to be faithful during his absence. Now here he is, after six years and counting, finally having the son he wants and obviously feeling good with himself and.........

Sweet Jesus! Soft succulent lips covers mine… and … and...and…..

To be continued.

ADENI

STORY 6

Chichi's Story

He sleeps soundly....a smile dancing around his lips just before bedtime (his bedtime) he received a call which he answered sweetly to and ended the call in less than ten seconds. While he tucked himself in bed, the phone beeped...text message? … A bbm ping? A whatsapp message? He read quickly and a happy beam spread all over him. Very happy smile spread on his face. He took a deep satisfied breath, obviously signifying contentment. He switched off his phone and fell fast asleep...a happy sleep.

He didn't even bother to say goodnight. I almost said kissed goodnight. Hahaha!!! Dreamer! Kiss! Kiss!! Kiss!!! Hmmm, that was donkey years ago. I don't even recall the feeling that comes with it.

I have been murdered over and over again by the man I call my husband. Eleven years in marriage. And up to this moment I speak, I can't pinpoint the problem with my marriage. I know there is a problem but I have no evidence to back my cause. And even if I do, who would listen to me?

Every one looks at the flashy cars I drive, the mega mansion I live in, the foreign vacations with the kids. My expensive wardrobe. (Point to note; it's a walk in closet that houses the most expensive designers in the world) my kids wear ONLY the very best. I have an array of staffs; domestic staff. I barely lift a finger and everyone jumps to the conclusion as to how lucky and blessed I am. Indeed and in truth I am blessed beyond words can describe.

But how do I explain that I am married but emotionally divorced. How? How do I tell the world of the cold unaffectionate life I live? The very lonely nights, alone in my bed. I feel so alone even when he lies next to me. And this is a man I so desperately love. I love him with everything that is in me. My soul, my body. I ache every minute for his touch; everything about him turns me on. He is my own blessing, my personal Viagra. My answer from heaven; for a life of bliss.

Night after night I long and ache for his touch, for his attention. Sometimes I pray for weeks on end that he should just make eye contact with me and I will sleep happily that night.

But none of my wishes as regarding my desires for him have been granted so far, even the simplest of all.

God!! How can I describe this pain? This rejection that is eating my soul away. What kills me more is knowing that what I long for, he gives out to another woman. Gosh! I feel light headed. I feel like fainting. It hurts so badly. I feel so hurt. So deeply hurt. God! When will this pain stop? How can I stop this daily, hourly and minute by minute misery that I feel? How God? I feel empty on the inside. I feel sharp pains in my chest and it's like my heart skips some beats.

I love him! I love him!! I love him!!! Who is this lady? Who is she that has thrown a stick in the wheels of my life? My hubby sees me as the mother of his children. The one that manages the home he lives in. I cook well, no great. I am in top shape. I take good care of myself. With the exorbitant monthly allowance that I am given, I dare not look drab. That will be the height of stupidity.

I made up my mind to investigate and look for a solution to whatever problem there is. God I am so willing to solve this.

When you put your mind to something, it's like events begin to work out positively to make you achieve that which you have set your heart to achieve.

I checked the time on my bedside alarm clock, two seventeen am! Hmmmmm!! I got up and move stealthily to his side of the bed, where he kept his phone while charging it. I had the password to his phone: or so I thought. I got there switched on the phone and keyed in the password and it opened.

I couldn't believe my luck. I tiptoed to the restroom. Sat down on the floor. Yes! Floor! I needed something to balance me properly for the earth shaking revelations, I know I am about to experience. My hands wet with perspiration, despite the very chilling air-conditioning in our room. My heart was beating fast. My pupils were dilated but I was determined to know the truth. I divided in. first stop was Bbm. One unread ping…. I thought damn! I opened.

Instantly I felt my spirit leave my body. I could hear my own thoughts very loud as I read the chat. It sounded like an echo, the whole room spinning very fast. It was like I was floating. I went to text messages from Zizi, then to whatsapp messages. I read enough to make me wet with desire-Stupid as it sounds. The conversation between them was solid. Very solid! They had a rhythm…they flowed; it was like they were two different part of a puzzle, so accurately fitted together. The relationship wasn't anything like erotic or sex based ….no….no…no… it has depth.

How else can I explain this? Even I unconsciously gave a seal of approval-these two were made for each other and soon they will be! I read their traditional marriage will be in summer. And I got to know that my hubby's greatest worry was how to break it to me. Even the way Zizi was also worried about me, touched me deeply. There was this sincerity about her-this confidence. She was one hundred percent certain, she has his heart but she was also concerned for me. She gave him a step by step procedure of how to handle the revelation saga. Am impressed! I give her a hi-five; cool plan!!

Eyes soaked. I moved stealthily back into bed. Kept everything back in place. Is it me or has the room suddenly got colder. I was shaken, the chats replayed in my minds' eye. Showing how my hubby kept repeating in all the chats how wonderful a wife I was. And how blessed any man would be to have me. He felt sad about the kids and feared a broken home may affect them. From the chats, I got the impression that he didn't plan to have a polygamous home, but according to him, he would die without Zizi.

He repeated often in their chat that he loves me. But theirs was overwhelming. She gave him three months to make me feel okay or else no wedding. They are taking a break sexually and promised to stay apart and not communicate. The plan is for him to bridge the gap between us, to try and win me over once more. Hmmmmm; like he lost me? Mtscheew!! Different thoughts kept going through my mind. Zizi's chats torment me- I almost like her too. She spoke of a perfect arrangement; as regarding the way we would live after their marriage. One week both ways. That is to say, he would spend one week with us and then the following week with her in continuous rotation. Outgoing to be shared equally, or where situations demand, we all go out together. She was satisfied to even have a man. "The man" she longed for all her life. Having lost her nineteen months old daughter and her hubby in a car accident. She was, according to her ready to settle for less, but she won't have dear hubby mistreat me to please her. Only if she knew of this past years of hell. Even on my wedding day, dear hubby was far away. So it's like I got everything cut out for me right from the very beginning.

What do I do now? Armed with this info that I have? I have to put emotions aside and think logically. I have for long figured out I always make wrong hurting decisions when I use emotions, painful lessons learnt.

Am turning thirty-nine in a few weeks, how do I fight this? I love this man God!! How do I live without him? Can I share him? Should I seek divorce and find new love? My kids? How do I ensure they get the best? Dear hubby had vowed in his chats to make it up to me-out of guilt he has been avoiding me for years. He was praying that God forgives him and makes everything a smooth transition. Zizi proposed he takes me to an island for my birthday... hmmm.... This Zizi sha!

As I tossed and turned, I felt the air-conditioning getting colder... "A trip to an island" The thought has me turned on. I am sure I would die if I am touched. I don't know I will react. It's been so very lonngg!

Suddenly, I felt warm hands, dragging me close. Jesus!!! Everything in me, exploded!! Chaos here and there. I struggled to keep everything together. Is that lips on my neck? Hot tongue on my ears? Blood of Jesus! He was murmuring. And wait! Is he sobbing? I sat up!! No, I jolted up! Is this all an act or what? Yes, I love him dearly but I won't have him play me.

He rested his head on my laps. I almost fainted. But kept very still. He started apologizing, I am sure He said 'I am sorry' a million times. He also threw in "forgive me" like a hundred thousand times. I thought of so many unfortunate women, who were thrown out of their marital home mercilessly, for another wife to step in. I thought about men who gave their wives adulterous name tags all with the aim of sending them packing and get a new wife. Should I be thankful for this apologies? At least I have been pre-informed through the chats. Should I be calm and watch everything play out?

To me divorce is a Not an option. But the past few years has been lonely and heart breaking. This sudden show of remorse and attention, plus renewed profession of dedication and care to the kids and I, should I embrace it? What are the alternatives? No D word. A marriage of solitude? Isn't this better than nothing I have endured these past years? I know I may be too trusting, but a part of me like Zizi already. I may sound foolish to some women out there but she's just like my hubby. And I understand why he loves her.

Dear hubby went on to give a very touching speech. He mostly felt guilty about hurting me. I was innocent of all this. I was a rebound. They had a messy breakup, which led to Zizi having a relationship where she got pregnant almost instantly. The guy was an angel and Zizi felt she had nothing to loose after all, dear hubby had broken up their engagement. He met me briefly after her wedding and he also seeing that I was good natured proposed to me and here we are. Eleven years later.

They both felt they would outgrow their teenage love and focus on their careers. They were in same industry and both doing excellently well, in fact coming together has boosted us financially.

Zizi has spent the last eight years of her life turning down suitors. She just could not click. I don't know the story of how they reconciled but here we are.

I listened and decided to let destiny play out, I am very close to turning forty...thirty-nine is almost here and here lies the man I love-No other....ONLY HIM!!! Would it be wise for me to leave? Here the Nigerian parable that "half a loaf of bread, is better than a full packet of small biscuit" came to mind!! Also "the devil you know is better than the angel you don't".

He told me, he plans to marry Zizi but he doesn't want it to be about that, he just wants to make me happy again- seeing that I deserve better. He says Zizi can't have children anymore, so he will be spending more time with me and the kids than at her side. Their relationship is not a threat to me, He emphasized. She hopes to adopt but that will be sorted out, He said

He asked me to say something. I said I just wanted to ask him one question. He asked me to go right ahead! I asked him if he knew what I feel for him. He said he knows that I love him completely, that He sees it in all I do and the thought that another shares his heart kills him, but he is just helpless, Zizi is a part of him that he has no idea what would happen if she leaves. He told me he loves me very much but he is not complete without her. Their love transcends the physical. But he promised to never ever hurt me. I said that's all I have to ask. That what he feels for Zizi is the same I feel for him. I would rather be with him than with any other man.

He held me and we cried together- loud sobs then silent tears. Then he searched for my face and kissed me. We had a steamy night-I died and resurrected then died again and resurrected... this man is my personal Viagra.

Fast forward months later...

My hubby married Zizi in a simple and quite ceremony, she lives in a different state now but not too far and manages the new branch office from there. We have had a few dinners together; pre and post wedding, she acted so nice. I didn't know what to make of it... but time will tell.

I had my birthday trip to an island in Europe. It was better than our honeymoon. I got pregnant from that trip...*laughing*...*winks*... it was all I hoped it would be.

I do not encourage polygamy neither do I condemn it... the three of us never planned to be in one but we have found ourselves in it.

Hubby spends ten days straight with us and the following five days with her. There are no complaints yet, everything is going smoothly.

My final words here, do what works best for you and don't be selfish when taking decisions- think of your kids and everyone to be affected.

I told myself, if I could endure all I passed through for years, then I am indeed strong! What kept me were the thought of my kids. They were psychologically and emotionally stable. They had the best of everything, I would sacrifice my personal desires any day for them.

If you feel like complaining, murmuring and getting depressed all day that could be your downfall but I would advise you to sit up. All those years I passed through pains, not a soul knew, I was emotionally unfulfilled! I acted happy; yes I was happy to some degrees; my kids were provided for extravagantly. I have a very comfortable... no, point of correction, choice cars, live in good environment and had all that makes live beautiful and I never seize to thank God!

As a matter of fact, recently, I was held in traffic, while I sat in my car silently listening to cool music I was distracted by noise of a siren (a moving convoy of cars where armed security personnel are strategically placed to guide an important personnel) I turned to look closely at the passengers and quickly recognized it was the hubby of a closed friend of mine. Her hubby married a second wife and moved out to live with this woman.

I noticed the son from the second marriage placed between both parents at the back of the jeep while the eldest wife who I happened to be close to, also has a son who from the day he was born, has not seen his father for up to one month cumulated in the little years of the small boys life. While this other woman's son get to spend every day with daddy. "What a world!" Nigerian cultures and traditions! When I saw that scene, something in my body turned- I can't place if it's my liver, my lungs, my stomach, my womb or intestine but I knew something in my body was in total disagreement with what my eyes saw. How will that lady cope? The thoughts that runs through her mind when her kids will ask "Mum, where is our daddy?" What will she tell him? That daddy is now married to an inconsiderate bitch who has selfishly refused to share? Tears rolled down my eyes as I watched this other lady smiling, chatting away with her dear hubby. Oblivious of the pain, the grief she has invited into the life of this other lady and her kids.

I ask myself, who is most guilty here? The lady who claimed another woman's hubby because our culture permits it or the man who so wickedly keeps away from his first family and dedicates time to just the second family? A man who definitely does not have a conscience and punishes an innocent woman he pursued, wooed and probably promised to give her the sun and the moon and then got married to her in church. This same woman he abandons emotionally, sexually and who knows what else. Yet he goes about very proud because culture permits all this brouhaha-he should have just put a knife on her throat. That lady in my opinion is nothing more than the house-help to her kids. But she's doing it without complaining, she still loves her husband no matter what. And she carries her cross quietly; "Suffering and smiling" like we say here in Nigeria.

Whenever I think of my dear friend and her misfortunate, I thank God for Zizi. For the fact that she's not as heartless and mean like this woman's mate.

So, if you are in a situation like mine, yours may not have turned out like mine- remember it took eleven long years of perseverance. So all I will say is, hold on some more because no matter how you think you are dealt the worse hand, I tell you today that it could be worse! We are in Africa. So many women, millions of them are not fortunate to have hardworking men like ours. They suffer from dawn to dusk. They have forgotten what it is like to be feminine. The men in their lives are nonchalant about issues that concern them and their kids. We have a man who remembers that the kids will eat, buy new clothes, go to school and have their general welfare taken care of- despite having Delilah's all about them-please be thankful!

Exalt God…

He is the one with Power!!

CHICHI.

STORY 7

Kite's Story

"I could hear voices though not audible. I find myself straining to gain focus and tried to listen to the voices around me. I could hear sounds from different machines, footsteps of a lot of people going up and about. Where was I? And God! The smell!!

Trying to open my eyes proved a Herculean task too. I didn't understand why. I kept trying hard.

"Can you see that? Did anyone also notice that?" That was definitely my mother asking. Oh my God! She's by my side! Why?

"Yes!! Yes!!! She's doing it again!!" Osonogbrugwe wakobiruoo!!! {Translation: God!!! I thank you! In my local dialect}

"Oh yes! I see!!" My baby sister screamed excitedly.

Finally I managed to open my eyes. Everywhere or everything rather was blurred. I shut them back very fast because it hurts really badly.

My mum must have noticed the stress I was going through with trying to open my eyes because I felt her hand on my cheeks, telling me in a low soothing voice to take it easy.

"Where am I?" I asked. Eyes still shut.

"You have been hospitalized… you have been in a coma for three days" my mum replied.

"What happened?" I queried

"There was another crisis…" answered my mum"

"Oh!!!" I answered, half expectedly … "Are my kids okay?

"Of course they are" mum answered "it's a good thing schools are on break, so they are coping quite well"

"It is well…" I said silently.

Tears falling down my cheeks, from my already sore and hurting eyes.

"Crisis!! Crisis!!! Crisis!!!!" I thought to myself

"Please try and relax darling, we will be back later" my mum said.

I could hear the door open and shut and soon I could hear rescinding footsteps of my mum and sibling walking down the hall way.

Left alone to myself, I wept bitterly, asking myself the one trillionth time how I ended up in this mess? Did my ancestors or forefathers do something bad? Am I reaping the harvest of the deed of a wicked grandparent? Did I offend someone in my past life? Is this a self inflicted curse?

How did marriage to Oke turn into a nightmare? How did the love-filled relationship during our courtship take a nose dive into something so awful?

Crisis!! Crisis!!! Crisis!!!!

Imagine the normalcy with which my mum said it. Everyone around me have come to label my fights with my hubby as crisis and due to the highly frequent occurrence of these fights (is it right to call it a fight? naaahhh!! Beatings suited my situation better-I was solely at the receiving end of the fights). The term crisis doesn't even carry the threat it's supposed to insinuate. Now, it's just like a fun name. Talk about abnormality.

My marriage of twelve years gives me so much heart ache and leaves me speechless at such times.

To a lot of people, especially those hard core Christians and religious marriage counselors, crisis are crisis, end of story. They are marital challenges. So therefore crisis is to be endured. Perseverance is the watch word. Crisis should be considered a challenge that should be endured with loads of fasting and prayers. Now, twelve years and counting I can't even put a figure to the number of fasting I have engaged in or the countless midnight prayers and hourly prayer sessions.

My marriage is now a prayer point to friends and family, even my neighbors. Anytime I walk by or drive through my street, I notice people staring at me eyes full with pity. Probably wondering how I cope.

Over the years, I have had quite a number of fractures, bruises and dislocations. I feel helpless. Our culture frowns at separation, divorce is a taboo. I ache all over. My heart is in turmoil. I have looked countless times in the mirror, I feel useless, worthless. Maybe if I was beautiful enough.

What can I do? The only way is the way out. And that is not happening. My parents will not hear of it. It has never happened in the genealogy of my family, both paternally and maternally. Everyone goes to marriage and remain there. No one wants to even listen to me.

I remember an aunt of mine telling me the last time

"At least Okiemute, you are eating this shit, with a diamond spoon. You have everything you desire, expensive cars, expensive cloths, expensive foreign trips and all. Women are dying to be in your position. After the fight, my love, put on your designer glasses, wear your designers clothes, enter your customized range rover evogue with elegant calculated steps (she cat walked to emphasize her point) and hit the town. Kite! Shop and shop and shop. Omor! {Slang for young lady} 'No look face oh!' {Trans; walk with head high}" your own better pass plenty women oh!"

She went on

"Yes, your hubby is a woman beater, hot tempered and violent but love am like that! No look the beating oh! Just bone! {Slang for over look} how many women get husband? How many women get moto? {Trans; A car} How many? Tell me? Some no get ordinary spook "{Trans; bicycle wheel}

She continued

"Plenty women wake up with hunger, as if that is not enough, they wake up to an empty kitchen, surrounded by kids, some up to four with hungry stomachs! Do you know the feeling? As a woman to stare into the hungry eyes of your beloved children and see hunger? And you know not how or where food will come from? Do you know the feeling of poverty? That feeling of helplessness? When you question the purpose of your existence? The reason for your breathing?"

"Some women are hypertensive from poverty 'wahala' {Trans; stress} when the milk is half; she begins to wonder where the resources will come from to replace it. Where? When baby food is half, she loses sleep. When the kids run temperature; she begins to panic because she knows too well the income of the family. The cheapest drugs she cannot afford. Some owe tuition for three terms straight. Some have to stop schooling despite the fact that they have very intelligent children. As a mother, you die a thousand deaths. Anytime you look at those innocent children, you ask yourself, why you didn't try harder. There's no pain like the pain of a mother watching her kids cry of hunger. No pain! No pain Kite!! At that stance, she could do anything, just about anything just to satisfy their hunger. Women are responsible for the fathers they give their children, so search and choose well. Else your kids will grow to insult you"

"Kite, I am your aunty, I don't like that Oke beats you to coma but my love I won't lie to you, endure the beating. So long as your kids have more than enough to eat, good schools to attend, clothes on their back and the extras; the expensive games, designer furnished private bedrooms, private swimming pool, French teacher, music teacher, foreign trips; bi-annually."

"Please I beg you Kite endure. Pay the price for these children. Not for yourself but for these children. I know the hell you are passing through. It is a messy situation. Oke will outgrow it; soon he will overcome his temper, but please for the sake of these children. Soon they will enter foreign colleges. When they have left your nest and safely in school, their future secured. That's when you will get down to business. If Oke has not changed by then. Hala me! {Trans; give me a call} I will give you tips on how to live life to the fullest as if you are a widow. By then you have little to lose. You will be free and have time to do as you wish. Am not saying you should leave your marriage please don't look at what others will say. Put wagging tongue behind you".

"Remember that red shoes you wore to my birthday party, the money for that shoe can finance a small scale business from start to finish. Millions of Nigerians queue outside microfinance banks to borrow money for business, how much? Thirty thousand naira (about one hundred and fifty dollars) and they spend good eight months working to pay back that cash with interest-ordinary thirty thousand naira you use for recharge card for your phone in a week! Or is that enough for you and the kids to eat when you go out for fun? Tell me now? Please oh! I won't advice you wrong. This is your marriage, seat tight, balance well, you won't leave. It is for better for worse."

I always reflect on the wisdom behind my aunt's words. Despite the fact that my spirit rejects the whole issue of this marriage, somewhere deep down in me I am touched by the naked truth of what my Aunt told me. What if I die?

"Hmmm..." I returned to my present state...

"Knock! Knock!!" The doctor stepped in.

"Mrs. Okiemute..." the doctor went on a long talk. He told me I would be released 'ONLY' when I get better and he suggested I see some women's rights initiative that assists domestically abused women. I politely told him no. He looked at me with disgust and confusion written all over his face. Even for a man, I guess He was fed up of seeing me frequently at his clinic, always dehumanized. And he left reluctantly.

I made a mental note to change hospitals or at least notify my close family just in case of future crisis (oh! God!)

Now alone to my thoughts once again, I closed my eyes, which still hurt so badly and tried to relax. My thought went back again to the conversation with my Aunt. She made sense if I look at it from different angles. Yes I have to be thankful for the life of luxury I enjoy. I mentally calculated the worth of everything I had on, just the small basic-jewelry, undies and slippers, to the basket of food, the cutleries

(I bought those cutleries from Dubai) it came to almost one quarter of a million naira (approximately one thousand five hundred dollars). Everything about me spelt money! I had more than I can ever spend-too much. Yes I thank God for my kids, they have everything, Oke went the extra mile to insure their future. Each had a Trust and Real Estate Overseas in their names, they had business where they own the major shares. If Oke suddenly passes, it won't change much financially. So many times when I am down, I get tempted to murder him, but I know that's wishful thinking. I am not wired like that. Oke is too powerful and he will never allow me live in peace if I dare leave him. Here in West Africa, the customary laws, favors the man a lot. I can't live without my children

I don't buy into what my aunty says despite the fact that she stated a lot of facts. What if I loose my life? Can't I also put me into consideration? What about my happiness? My emotional and physical well-being? I can't even think. No strength to. But one thing is for sure; Oke will be my husband forever. No separations, no divorce.

My village will not even let me (they benefit greatly from my spouse), my family, my friends all of them would declare me mad. To run and leave all these billions to where? I can imagine the statements and comments if I left. And my kids, I would die first before leaving them. I wouldn't even have put my feet outside the door before another woman runs in. Another woman whose mission will be to put my kids out of the way and put whatever children she has in strategic positions. Am sure my family may even suggest giving him one of my sisters or cousins, because they wouldn't want to lose what they benefit from Oke. See what riches can do? Despite Oke's billions he has told everyone that polygamy is not happening. He has stated it right from a very tender age that he will never practice polygamy. It's going to be Okiemute and Oke forever. So, Case closed.

I can feel sleep coming…

"Thank God…" I murmured and allowed sleep carry me away.

Life goes on…

KITE.

STORY 8

Temabo's Story

I stood and watched Ovuokio slammed the door behind him as he angrily walks out. I stood still but everywhere else was spinning. Yes, spinning very fast.

"What is going on?"

"Is this for real?"

I looked down at my protruding belle. I am almost seven months gone. I couldn't put together all that is happening. I tried to be calm and turned around looking for the best place to sit and catch my thoughts. I changed my mind and decided to lie down on my bed.

My mind went back to early in the year; I was about three months pregnant when my mother called me for a heart to heart talk. I met her seating at the head of the dinner table. So I sat at the opposite end. She asked me if during the period of separation from my husband, I didn't sleep with any man. I told my mum to stick her nose only where it concerns her. How does my sex life, have to do with anything?

She calmly told me that there's a reason for her asking and she has no intent of poking her nose into my private life but she needs to be sure I am not at risk.

I was like, "at risk of what 'male'?" {Pronounced mah leh –southern Naija slang for mum}. She then went on to explain something I thought I heard once or twice but never paid any attention to.

She went on to explain that in our tradition (my mum happens to be the same tribe as my husband; both are from the same village) when a lady gets married, dowry is been paid traditionally.

I chipped in-"in my case, twenty-five naira and so?"

An alarm went off in my head. Why is she going into this?

"That twenty-five naira you just said signifies and binds together a lot."

"Like?" I chipped in again.

I noticed my mum struggling to be calm, I could see she was saddened by whatever she so believed in and I could smell her fear literally. This woman is serious hey! I decided to shut up and listen.

But my mind went way back further to some few years back when I was pregnant with my son. That was my first pregnancy. We were seated on the dining table facing each other like this at the two extremes. She brought up this traditional stuff and started by saying I needed to be circumcised before I give birth. She went into a long talk about the reasons for it. I swear I can't place my hand on one thing because I wasn't listening. But I can still remember a statement of hers that made me scream.

After much talk she said, "Ok if you don't want, no problem but na you go short sha!" {Trans; I would be the one at a loss}

I retorted sharply, "Short, how???"

"Yes now, short!!! She emphatically went on to explain. "When you are circumcised now that you are pregnant by your husband, it is a thing of great pride (huhh!?) After circumcision, for the next few days you will be dressed in wrapper and gorgeous beads and Owhara {a red powdery stuff} will be rubbed all over your body all through this time. Whenever you go out, people will be giving you cash gifts and praying and singing praises for you".

"There are two types, the one they do 'IN' and the one they do 'OUT'. The one of 'INDOOR' is hidden like a secret. It's only when you apply the Owhara that people will know you have been circumcised".

"So you just walk about in Red from head toe, clad only in a wrapper tied around your chest…"

I started to criticize but she wouldn't let me finish.

"No…no…no…. the lady also wears gorgeous beads depending on the status of her family. She goes about carrying an umbrella. She also has a young girl with her. A beautiful young girl, may be around ten – thirteen years of age. The little girl is also rubbed with 'Owhara' from head to toe, and ties wrapper on her chest with beads and also holds her own umbrella, just like the newly circumcised lady".

My mum stood up and started walking slowly taking one step slowly after another, almost like she was on a runway doing catwalks. I watched in shock.

She was beaming with pride, as she cat walked around the dinner table, obviously reliving her own circumcision experience. She walked about our living room and continued her tale

"People would look at you with envy! People…"

"ENVY????" I shouted in shock and immediately started laughing… my mum paused to look at me in wonder.

"Yes now, Envy! It is a thing of great pride!" she replied.

"To have your female genitals cut off! No Clitoris! To castrate you, to render you useless for life and you say envy?" I couldn't believe my ears.

"Castrate? Useless??" my mum stood perplexed. To her, I must be one very ignorant young lady. She shook her head. I kind of felt she was feeling sorry for me. Yes me! Can you imagine?

I went on to explain "mum there's nothing good about having your clitoris cut off. Why? How would one enjoy sex?"

"The point exactly!!" she said "women are not meant to enjoy sex too much. That piece of flesh makes women promiscuous. A woman that likes sex too much becomes a problem to herself, her husband and everyone. If not properly managed she could cheat and that is the biggest disgrace of the Urhobo woman-to be an unfaithful wife. The consequences are great!"

"What consequences?" I asked "Anyways, so the reason for this piece of flesh been cut off is to control the sexual appetite of the woman – No! Not control, they KILL IT!!!"

"Yes, they kill it. A circumcised woman can stay for years, long years without having sex"

"And who benefits from that?" I queried

I continued, "In effect, what you mean is that, it was done to the betterment of the man. So that in the case where he has to travel for extended periods, he would know that the wife would seat, leg closed and wait faithfully for him without having the urge to commit adultery or in the case where a man marries two or more wives he can do as he pleases right? The way I see it;

One – the women won't get jealous, why would they get jealous about what they don't enjoy? Sex becomes a duty. The men don't need to please the women; all she's got to do is have her bath, then present her body.

Then – two – he can go around many women as he wishes and it doesn't matter if he takes three months to get to the turn of number one again because without a doubt his 'stick(wife),' his lifeless object would be there waiting the way he left it. This is all a man's idea and the women stupidly bought into it. God forbid!"

"God forbid?" mum asked not believing her ears. Did she really think she could convince me to do this?

"Yes! God forbid! I can never have my daughter circumcised or myself. My husband wouldn't even allow it. Do you know the joy and pleasure that piece of flesh brings?"

"Tell me..." mum said

"No way!! Am not discussing oral sex or fore play with you Mahleh". I walked out.

Now am back at the dining table. In the Present, anxiously waiting to hear another of those traditional jargons. But this time my mum didn't look at all excited the way she was with the circumcision issue. I perceived fear this time. And it kind of scares me too.

She went on to explain that the normal traditional marriage rites performed on the day of the traditional wedding, like the pouring of local gin on floor to ancestors has great significance.

I reminded her that there was no alcohol at my wedding and no gin was poured on the floor. She told me that it doesn't matter, that a dowry was paid by my husband's family. And the point to note is that as long as this dowry (twenty-five naira - in my case) still remains in the hands of the bride's family and has not been returned that the marriage is still bound by tradition. If the woman has any contact or dealings with another man, it could be just kissing, petting or sex. Even collection of money or gifts is frowned upon and the consequence is great.

"Consequences like?" I asked?

"Please let's just know if we will even have to go into all that…"

"Mahleh please what consequences?" – I asked determined to know.

"In your case where you packed all your luggage and left his house, even relocated to another country for a year plus, the case is understandable."

"Mum please speak up, stop trying to beautify the whole issue" - I stressed.

"Yes, if you happen to have sexual relations with any man. There are traditional rites that needs to be performed by your husband's family for you before you can step foot into your husband's house."

"Traditional rites like? And for what?"

"To appease the gods and ask for their forgiveness"

"Which gods? The forefathers?" I asked "Oh! The bunch of dead guys!"

"TEMABO!!!!' mum exclaimed

"Yes now" I continued "So after tormenting women when they are alive, they continue when dead. Please, please, please, maleh, I don't want to hear all this non-sense…" I stood up "it's my body, I have needs. I separated from my husband for a reason. Didn't he meet with other women too??"

"Men are not held by tradition; they are free to do what they want"

"Oh! Really?"

"You see why circumcision is good? If you were circumcised, your body wont need anything. Temabo, it's just only a year you separated from your husband. Are you saying you did something?" her eyes were all watered up. "Women can stay for long years without sex... why the rush Temabo? This is bad oh! Your husband's family will ask oh!"

She was sobbing by now "I don't want to loose my child or my grandchild please! You are pregnant, if you did something, talk now, we have to serve the gods for you or you won't be able to give birth successfully..."

"God forbid... nobody put this baby in my womb and no one has a say in the birth of this baby"

"Temabo! You don't understand ... please tell me, if you had any relationship, so we know what to do. I am your mother, please talk to me. I am on your side. It doesn't matter what happened, everyone will understand that you left your husband and probably thought you would never make up and you moved on..."

"This is rubbish mahleh... my private life is not for public..." I stated but was cut short.

"Temabo, think of your child. Think of the baby in your womb. Think of your own life, your glorious destiny and consider the man who has loved you non-stop all of these years...your husband"

"Mahleh, please, let's end this now... please enough! End of discussion please. I need to sleep! This is ridiculous!" I stood in disbelief and walked away, leaving her to her tears.

Now months later, what my mum warned me about has reared its ugly head again.

Ovuokio and I have always been friends. That's one beautiful part of our relationship. Ovuokio is a good five feet eight inches tall, is dark skinned and a little on the chubby side, handsome and of a very calm temperament. He is so quiet everyone tells me I am blessed to be married to him. I remember a friend of mine asking me if he was ever able to make me angry. I told her to come borrow him for a week. He is five years older than me. He is a businessman and the first son of his mother.

While I am the very ambitious type. The go-getter. The talkative. My mum says I talk nonstop like a radio from early childhood and they all wondered how I keep up. That doesn't mean I am a gossip.

I am just the type that enjoys conversations and when I decide to talk about something I am passionate about, I like my 'audience' to understand me in every way, so I explain a lot.

I am not tall and neither am I short. I am very chubby and can be termed plus-size. I am very well educated and I have great love for books. I also love to write and can cook very well. And yes for the part I have been avoiding; I am beautiful…in my own way, yes, I am beautiful. I have got these very pretty eyes, in fact that's what my hubby loves most about me. He says he gets lost in them.*winks*. I also have a very small mouth, crowned with cute lips and cute pointed nose set in a round face. I am chocolate skinned as we say here in naija. I am a businesswoman, into interior decoration.

Our marriage has been like every other marriages', all faced with their unique problems. We have a son. Our only child. I stormed out when I couldn't take in some of the issues I was faced with. After our separation and we got back together-I got pregnant almost immediately. I was still at my father's house when I had the other conversation with my mother. So many painful issues after and now we live together in a new apartment.

Unknown to me, my hubby's family has been on his neck about this matter, because according to tradition; I have not been cleansed. And for him to be sleeping with me under the same roof and eating my food is deadly. It's a ticking time bomb- borrowing the words of one of the elders of his family. So his family has been scared for his life. But in his usual quiet ways of approaching issues, he kept it from me.

But as my pregnancy draws to its end, the tension has intensified. My mum scared that I won't make it out of the delivery room alive and my in-laws scared that their son may die. It has been Chaotic. We have spent many sleepless nights on this matter. My Hubby cajoled me to know if I had sexual relations with another man. I told him yes of course I did but I maintained my stand of not performing any rites.

My mum would call me on the phone begging endlessly. I would remind her of my stand as a Christian and performing traditional rites that includes killing of an animal was against my religious beliefs.

She kept saying "Temabo, give to Caesar, what belongs to Caesar! Forefathers are deadly! They are merciless!"

Ovuokio, my hubby has now gotten tired of begging me. This morning, he repeated that he was tired of begging me for my own good!! He said after the rites, his life, that of our son, and the life of our unborn child is also secured. He also said, I would be permitted to be in my marital home in peace. We will all be living again together as family peacefully. Without these rites, so many things could go wrong.

Can you imagine? He was begging me to perform the rites for my own good. For my own good? I can't seem to get that line off my mind. I have cried and cried- I don't know if I have any tears left in my tear duct (gland).

I have asked around about this rites and what it entails. I was given a comprehensive breakdown.

I would have to face a panel (comprising of members of my hubby's family) with my hubby to present our case. In that panel, I would be asked to say my stance. My hubby will be excused as my confessions are not to be made in his presence. I would then be asked to tell them how many men I slept with. At this stage, they just need the numbers. Then they decide my case, if I am to be welcomed back into the family.

If the decision is positive, a list of items will be given to me, to bring for the rites. I would be warned sternly not to use any money from my husband's pocket. Not a dime of his should be added to the money needed to buy these items. And I was told that in my case, since we live together, I would be asked to stop cooking for my husband and have no sexual relations till the rites are performed.

The whole theory is quite a wide one. Let me try and enumerate.

It is the law {One I was obviously ignorant of, and am sure a lot of ladies too} that when a woman who has dowry paid on her head, like me, for whatever reasons, has sexual relations with another man, she's frowned upon by the god's. But there's a catch, if she lives under her husband's roof and still cooks for him, tragedy is knocking. Soon the hubby will fall sick, so sick that no medicine can cure him. This sickness will lead to questions been asked, and if the family of the man is traditionally wise, they will seek traditional assistance fast. Consultation would go on to reveal the deeds of the wife.

In such cases, the woman would be asked to confess and save the life of her husband. She will have to count the names of all the men she slept with. And after that, sacrifice of a live goat will be done with all other items the wife will be asked to bring. Cleansing will be done and she will be considered clean again.

In a case where the woman refuses to confess or the family of the man could not act fast, the man would loose his life. If the man is the spiritually strong type, the death would bounce to the children till the lady confesses her sins. Also a woman that gets pregnant after adultery and fails to cleanse herself faces a difficult labor – a prolonged and painful one that leads to questions been asked why or she would on her own confess out of anguish. If the rites are performed fast, she will put to birth. But if not she would lose her life but the baby would survive. If she escapes through operation, the baby's life would be saved and after the birth of the baby, birth complications will occur and the lady will definitely loose her life. Autopsy can give whatever reason they see but the bottom line is she's paid a price for her wicked and evil deed.

And this has nothing to do with whether the hubby of this particular lady is from the same part of the country as she is. The same goes for her. They are still other sides to it that I didn't explore. Just wanted to know what would happen in my own case, now I know.

Still in bed, weak from the emotional stress- I have been hospitalized thrice from high blood pressure. What do I do? My father who is not from this part of the country has put a deaf ear. He plays dumb and sticks to his religious belief. Let me not go into how his nonchalant attitude affects me. This is my cross, my mum volunteering herself and I alone will have to carry it. I want to do it willingly not coerced. Something in me has not totally bought into the whole idea. When and if it does, I will do it.

My son is in school. I am home alone, baby kicking, I stood up and proceeded to go make a snack. While putting together the snack, my mind went to work. And I thought to Google and find out if such things exist elsewhere and what is the reaction of people to it.

I picked up my laptop and googled. A line caught my attention. I clicked and read through! Wow! Seriously? Somewhere in the Eastern part of Nigeria, a man was killed by his ancestors for knowing about his wife's infidelity and trying to cover it up. I sat down and read through.

As the article stated, the part of the country where the deceased man originated from, frowns on infidelity by women. In this part, the woman is called for questioning, she is then sent to the market/village square (A densely populated part of the village known for a lot of activities) At the village square, she's to go naked, (by naked, I didn't get it clearly, if she's to remove all article of clothing or just partial) stand at the village/market square and confess her evil deed. She would name the man/men and where and how they did it. She would then walk through the town, and end up at the town shrine where cleansing will take place.

If the man, the spouse of this woman, is aware of her cheating, by which ever means whether she confesses to him or not, the fact that he is aware and kept quiet and do not notify his family members has harsh consequence. He may decide to forgive and save his family and children especially from the ridicule and trauma.

What is the essence of the punishment where the whole village will get to see her naked? Is it that they don't physically touch her with their hand that makes the difference? Everyone will see her privates. Then she will have to go back to her hubby. Isn't that intensifying the whole issue? That one man or two men who slept with her saw her nakedness and all the villagers seeing it-which is worse? I don't get it. No wonder the men (husbands) get to hide it. Any way my thoughts or opinion doesn't and will never count here. And it states here that the actions of the gods happens very fast. Eish!! That's some very angry and very hardworking forefathers.

I sat down thinking, willing myself to see things objectively and not emotionally.

Yes, I left my hubby. I was the one who left and when we made up, I returned. I had two serious relationships and a few other flings, all not adding up to the number of fingers on one hand. But the deed was done.

Temabo focus! Please focus!! I willed myself.

I made the decision to return. No one forced me. If I had known this would happen, I wouldn't have returned, that I am sure. Or am I? My hubby's family are all crying out that they don't want a death in their family, that they can't loose their son. And they are very concerned because of the way my hubby has stubbornly stuck to me. And according to their beliefs, their son is digging his own grave by living under the same roof with me, eating my food and having sexual relations with me.

Point to note; my in-laws are highly educated people and well placed in the society. But tradition they insist is tradition.

What do I do? What is the issue holding me back? Is it the rite in itself as in to kill a goat and pray to the dead? Or the ridicule... ridicule. What ridicule? I feel no shame whatsoever. No remorse. Yes, I slept with someone not my husband, but my conscience was cleared. I was never coming back. I was separated. I had no pin in his house. I didn't even do change of name for the period of time we were married. All documents I had prior marriage remained the same. Only that twenty-five naira was what was holding me back as at when I moved on with my life. If I had known I would do this sacrifice, I may never have returned. Thank God I didn't know. I wouldn't be pregnant with this precious child I carry now.

I started a conversation with myself.

"Temabo, so what's the way forward? The ridicule doesn't bother you. In fact, I don't feel it. Can't feel it. Even if I have to stand before the whole family of my hubby and do whatever it is, they desire. So what's holding me back from doing this? My hubby's family are scared for their son, my mum is concerned about me. She can't loose her daughter to manipulations by ancestral spirit during child birth – her beliefs."

"So what's the hold up? Let me stop doing this running around in circles and face reality; who stands to lose? Since I am positive nothing can happen to me, what about those that depend on me?

Your hubby whose life is threatened. There are evil people all around. If you don't do this and something bad happens whether from the ancestors or not, it would be attributed to him being killed from my Unfaithfulness (huh?! Unfaithfulness? Who was unfaithful? Me? I refuse to buy into that term. Hellooo world! We were separated, Puuleeaaseee!!!) Temabo focus!!"

"So what is my gain in loosing a hubby? And my children becoming fatherless? What about my kids? Hmmmmm......."

"My hubby is a rare gem. I can't bear the thought of loosing him. Or my children becoming fatherless."

"So Temabo, what's the verdict? What's our decision?"

"I AM GOING TO DO THIS!!"

I do not know the reasons for this outrageous law but it's clear that I broke the law and am caught in between. And ignorance is not an excuse. I will do it. It's quite unfortunate that I am from West Africa where ridiculous laws are practiced.

Despite the pretense of civilization, people still stick to their traditional beliefs. Despite the emergency of churches on every street, people still go behind close doors to serve traditional idol and ancestors.

I picked up the phone and called my mum and told her I am ready and willing. She didn't say anything and I hung up. Why was she silent? Was it shock? Anyway, I decided to send hubby a text. I was not in the mood for his sarcastic statements. Not now. I have very fast fingers, just like my mouth. Text sent. I decided to take a nap and await the ritual.

Days later....

The deed has been done. I mean the sacrifice and cleansing has been done for me. I heard it's something one does not repeat, or talk about. That what went on at the family home, where the rites took place is not to be discussed. It's a taboo to discuss the events of that day to someone who was not there. It was also said that no one can point a finger at me and say any rude remark; the consequences of such actions are great.

Well, I sincerely do not care if anyone has anything to say or not. In fact I invited one or two close persons to come witness my "serving" the forefathers of my husband's house.

After that phone call to my mum, she and my relative from her own side swung things into motion. And soon I was summoned with my husband. We were asked to describe to them in detail what happened and how we came to the conclusion that we need to serve the gods. We told our story and right there in the presence of all, my hubby was asked to leave for he didn't need to be present when I confess and he will never get to know what I confessed to. No matter the number of men I slept with, the how and the where, these details will be kept away from him for life.

I was asked to name the number of men I slept with so as to know how to fine me. I told them and they went on to name some items.

A live native goat (super size)
1 Bunch of unripe plantain
3 large tubers of yams
Different condiments
1 bottle Local gin
1 bottle foreign gin
10 liters of Native palm wine
Cartons of Can drinks
Cartons of bottled Water

We were also responsible for buying all the necessary items to cook and serve the food. Even soap to wash the pots and towel to wipe their hands. Down to firewood to cook the food, matches to light the fire, and to sponge to wash the pots. My hubby was not to contribute a dime or see these items with his eyes.

My mum was super ready and she got these items with admirable speed. I don't know if I am breaking any laws by saying these things, but I feel no shame, so I don't think anyone should.

My mum bought everything to the latter. I was also fined, not peanuts mind you. Aside been fined, I was called in and asked if I collected cash from any man. From the man/men I slept with. I told them it's a cashless economy outside Nigeria, but spoke about a cash gift from a dear friend who is not my lover. I was fined again for collecting cash from a guy even while a dowry was on my head.

My mother was also fined, for being a native of the land and not warning me against breaking the laws of the land. She was also fined for being my accomplice in packing my stuff from my matrimonial home and for also opening her home to welcome me back from my hubby's house. Ridiculous right? Women are not suppose to return back home from marriage no matter what!

I was called in to the room where the meeting is held after the first inquisition about the cash, to come face the forefathers and serve the gods proper. I stood before a small shrine with blood oozing fresh from the goat head that has just been cut off. I was told to stand before them and confess my sins. Call the names of the men and how it went down and ask for forgiveness from my in-laws ancestors and beg them not to kill my husband, son or unborn child. I did exactly that. I held a glass of local gin and they prayed for me.

After the prayers, I was declared whole and cleansed and brand new and asked to go home to my husband and give him a nice time.

Me, I was all smiles, ear to ear. I didn't have any problems with the ritual, once I had put my mind to it… It was easy and fun. I told the names of my partners and did the begging. It went smoothly. Everyone was satisfied. I was asked to leave.

My mum was asked to pay the man who would cook the food for them. There's going to be a big party afterward. The goat was huge, enough yams and plantain, cartons of alcoholic and non alcoholic drinks. I even heard text messages were sent out to people to come party with them; Ovuokio's wife has served their forefathers and there was more than enough for Sunday jollification.

At the end of that sunny Sunday afternoon, my mum was set back a good amount of tens of thousands of naira. When you add all the items she bought, she spent in my calculation up to seventy thousand naira (five hundred dollars plus) but I didn't ask for her the figure, because I knew, the cash was not a problem for her but to preserve the life of her daughter and her unborn grandchild.

Mind you, my hubby couldn't be present at this meeting; he can't know what went on there. If he asked even, no one will tell him. Those who were present and heard the number of men I called can't say what they heard to another living person. It is a taboo. That doesn't bother me, if they like they can broadcast it life on the local TV station.

I did what I did to achieve a goal. My goal! And I have achieved that successfully.

I don't know about others out there, or how they battled their own issues of serving the fore fathers of their in-law's house. But I want to say, this things are real. You hear them like folk lore... People act like it doesn't happen, but it does.

The day of your traditional marriage, while you are inside changing from one outfit to another, realize what it is you are actually getting yourself into. I did serve to cut off the possibilities of any foul play. Despite the fact that I was separated from my hubby and out of ignorance did stuff. I was not let go. I had to pay the price. It was expensive but my mum could afford it. It was meant to be very humiliating. But I felt none of that. Up to this day as I am speaking, I feel no guilt! Yes none. And that's because whatever I did, I did with a clear conscience.

This is Africa, this is West Africa and Nigeria for that matter. Ask well about cultures and traditions before you throw yourself into a mess your family won't be able to recover from.

A word is enough for the wise…

Temabo

STORY 9

Nnenna's Story

The putrid odor danced its way into my nostrils, unwelcomed. I jolted out of sleep. I sat up and tried to remember where I was.

Oh! My parent's home. I recollected. I was in my bed downstairs in my old bedroom, next to my sister's room.

"Sister!!"

"NNENNA!!!"

I jumped out of bed and ran straight for her room. I bashed in without knocking and ran to her bed side. I looked into her face, turned her to look into her eyes, to check her breath. Yes! Thank God! She is still with us. Nnenna has made it through another night.

It's a heartbreaking experience watching your once bubbling sister become a lizard. Yes that's how best I can describe her. She has no resemblance whatsoever to a human being. Only her skeleton, wrapped around by stretched skin, if I can call it that. She's in a pretty bad shape. We have taken her to different specialist hospitals and nothing could be done for her. She was flown abroad twice and returned just the same.

About three weeks ago, out of desperation, my grandma and her relatives went in search of answers. And they found it.

It was discovered that my sister took a blood oath with her first love Emeka. Things would have been fine if they stuck together but sadly that was not to be. My parents battled with Nnenna for years to let go of Emeka who was a no-gooder. She had stubbornly refused. Now we know why.

But the Irony of it all was that Emeka is a chronic flirt and has slept with countless women. The oracle said, the answer lies with Emeka and that after speaking with Emeka, if he agrees to break the oath, then the two of them should be brought back and the oath broken.

Emeka was confronted and he made some shocking revelations. He said the oath was one-way. That, while they both pierced their thumb in other to lick their blood, he didn't lick hers. That is, Emeka did not lick my sister's blood, but made her believe he did.

My sister on the other hand drank not sucked his own pierced thumb. And with the assumption on Nnenna's part, they both went ahead and declared before the god's that whoever slept with another human except them let an incurable disease what will defy all treatment be the penalty to be paid by the defaulter.

My sister has decided to tell her story today and will start any minute now, but let me share a little bit about our lives as family and about my older sibling Nnenna.

We are a Christian family of four that's equally divided; we are two girls and two boys. Nnenna came first, followed by the two boys then me.

We were an average family, early in life. We were not poor, but we couldn't be called rich. Daddy was a civil servant, now retired. Mum a petty trader. We attended public schools but we all got scholarships into private universities. My brothers, one a doctor and the other an engineer got foreign scholarships to go further. The engineer to do his masters, he made a first class and from there proceeded to do his doctorates. The doctor got internship in a world-class hospital in America, where he is now a resident pediatrician. They both ensured that our status was changed from average to way above average.

Nnenna … had a bright future ahead of her, or so we thought.

Let her tell her own story.

As for yours sincerely, I won an essay competition in my level 1 of studying mass communication and was transferred to a foreign University. After my education, I did my masters and returned to Nigeria to work as dictated by the terms of my scholarship. After four years of community service, I applied for Canadian Resident Permit and was granted with my hubby and two kids.

I had to return home, when I was informed of my sister's misfortune. My parents are both retired but my dad now runs a haulage business. My mum too travels to source for goods and sells them from home. We have a very big garage where she uses as her sales outlet. She sells diverse goods, depending on what catches her fancy when she travels. It could be households, (which includes a lot from cooking utensils to interior decorating items to souvenirs) she sells wrappers, laces etc.

My brothers built a modest seven bedroom duplex for our family. I was the one who stayed a bit with them, during the years after my return from England; Nnenna married Emeka while in her youth service. I personally am surprised that he let her go through with University. It was a constant struggle with Nnenna and my parents. They fought every other time. It was my parent's resistance to Emeka's daily marriage proposals that made Nnenna finish school.

Emeka refused to do anything productive with his life. Nnenna lived in fear of him. She was ten years my senior but I saw the constant fear in her eyes and her body language could not be mistaken. She was trapped in something beyond her. I used to think maybe it was the sex. Emeka has the body of a Greek god. He was sleek, suave, very tall, dark and breathtakingly handsome.

Nnenna on the other was a beauty queen. She won all beauty contests from primary school up to university level. She won all her schools beauty pageant. Our sitting room is filled with different awards and tiaras; Miss Hostel, Miss Department, Miss Faculty, Miss this and that. She was a charmer, soft spoken and calm. (Was? Am already talking about her in the past tense. That's because all those years seem like ages ago. When you see my sister now, you can hardly place her to the award winning beauty queen I have been talking about. She is nothing but a shadow of her former self and it kills me slowly)

I don't know how she managed to graduate from accounting with honors, second class upper to be precise with all the constant boyfriend wahala {Trans- stress}

Well, I wasn't around for almost eight years and didn't witness a lot of strange things that went on.

Let's hear from Nnenna.... She's ready for you.

"I met Emeka while in my junior secondary school. His school was invited to come participate in my schools inter-house sports competition. I was in junior secondary school two (II), I was turning thirteen and represented my house- yellow house in the beauty consent which I won as usual.

He was in the four hundred meters race and four hundreds relay race which he won effortlessly for his school and set a new record. He was seventeen.

It was easy to fall in love with him. He was tall, very handsome features, very charming smile and an overall great charisma. I fell in love at first sight, he did too.

We exchanged postal address and lived to wait for each others letters. Through our communication, we found out we were from the same village but different quarters. It was thrilling to realize we were so closely bonded. We had same culture and traditions guiding and binding us. He soon wrote his final exams and passed excellently, while I went into Junior Secondary School three. Later that year, we met in the village for the yearly Christmas events; those were the best days of my life.

I won the maidens beauty contest to the delight of Emeka, who also won the male category. He was four years my senior and was perfect.

I often wonder how I managed on stage, because I am the worst kind of introvert. I revel in my own privacy. I adore and do not joke with my alone time. At such times, I pamper myself; I take good care of myself by taking supplements, eating loads and loads of fruits that makes my fair complex1ion glow and due to been always indoors. I stay away from the sun, the sun and I are enemies. I rarely go out in the sun except need be and I always arm myself with an umbrella. My skin glowed, my hair so black and very long, I used homemade recipes, right from my mother's pantry. My eyes and teeth where sparkling white, I do not do alcohols. At thirteen, I was already five feet, eight inches tall, straight legs, nice physique I could be easily mistaken to a mixed breed 'mulato' as they call them. God was good to me. I had a queenly posture, everything about me spoke volumes. I could pass for royalty. I am soft spoken, I have never quarreled with anyone in all my years of life. I was not capable of malice. I couldn't loose control or loose my temper. I couldn't hold a grudge.

I knew early in life that I had a ministry, one that has to do with caring for people. God rightly positioned me to be the first child. I had big dreams for my family. I was made senior for a reason, through me; doors of breakthrough will be opened for my siblings. We are a close knitted family and we were taught to focus very early in life. I heard the word focus so many times a day; it was ingrained to my internal hard drive.

Life went smoothly till I met Emeka. Even after then, life went smoother. The thrills of being in love, the excitement and anticipation was awesome

Emeka and I suited each other perfectly, but unlike me, he was the last child and only son in a family of seven. He had six beautiful sisters ahead of him. I used to think that was to my advantage because as I thought, it would make him treat other women like queens, since he has a bunch of them as sisters. Only if I knew better back then, I would have avoided a lot of pains.

Ten months after meeting Emeka, and enjoying his attention and wooing, I agreed to be his girl friend.

New Year's Eve, at the village square, Emeka told me of his plans of going to an aviation school in the North and won't be back for a while.

He took my hand and we strolled to the village shrine, to a sacred tree where lovers take oath and engrave their names on the trunk of the tree.

We got there and Emeka knelt down and asked me to be his wife. He promised to give me the world and loved me like no other. He would be a pilot and earn big and take our 'boys' and I on countless vacations around the world. He would buy me a big mansion, I would have cooks and stewards and chauffer. Emeka promised he would put the world at my feet.

Right there after I accepted, he stood up and brought out a pen knife and engraved Emeka loves Nnenna on the tree.

Then he asked us to seal the engagement with an oath. He won't touch any girl till marriage, and the same applies to me. No man/woman will ever touch us or have any sexual encounter with us. We are virgins, pure and undefiled that is how we will be to each other till death do us part. Then, Emeka went on to say any one that breaks this oath will be dealt with a combination of the worst ailments that will defy all medical treatments. I went on to agree and we both licked each others blood or so I thought.

Emeka left for Aviation School located in the Northern part of Nigeria. I cried and cried, missing him badly. He never failed to write me.

Three years flew by, I went on to win more pageants.

On the day I wrote my final exams, I got a letter from Emeka, congratulating me and wishing me well. He told me he would see me later that year at Christmas. I quickly counted, that would be six months' time. I waited in anticipation.

Six months flew by and December was here. After my exams, to avoid been idle, my dad registered me for a six months computer programme.

At the computer school, I met Ebuka, a graduate of Computer Science. He was one of our tutors. From the moment he laid his eyes on me, Ebuka was lost. He didn't give me any room; he professed his love day and night. I told him I was betrothed. He couldn't and refused to believe me. Since I was not the defensive type, I went ahead and made friends with Ebuka. We became inseparable, I told him of Emeka all the time but I never mentioned oath- it was our secret.

December came and gone, no Emeka. I was heartbroken. Meanwhile, Ebuka traveled every day from his village to see me.

Which was quite a distance. The daily hassles, didn't bother him and everyone in my family, especially my dad soon grew fond of Ebuka. He was a computer whiz kid. A first class material and was awaiting the result of the aptitude test he wrote in Shell- a British multinational company. He told me he was sure he would ace it.

My brother, the engineer formed a close tie with Ebuka and they too became inseparable. Ebuka had access to the internet and exposed my brothers to the opportunities that were provided by the internet. He soon started writing applications for both of them online-applications for foreign scholarships for postgraduate studies.

In January, Ebuka got a scholarship to go for his masters abroad, he left almost immediately.

Valentine's Day came, I had turned seventeen. It's been four years now that I met Emeka. My results were out and I passed- an average but okay result. I could gain admission with it. That was what was paramount to me.

I also took JAMB- the university matriculation examination and was waiting anxiously for my result.

Point to note. My parents and I have been getting proposals for my hand in marriage from home and abroad. The request came in quite a number, due to my calm nature, clean record, family devotion to one another, I was held in high esteem. Top rated among the maidens in my village, I was a prize to behold. I was loved. I am one of those few persons who are able to get quite well with a lot of people. And I also suspect that because of my beauty and outstanding resume, a lot of people were partial to me. They let me get my way every time and are happy to do things for me. I get gifts every day. I get a lot of freebies too. It's not unusual for me to walk into a supermarket and do some shopping, then at the pay counter get to see someone begging to pay for my items.

But I chose to stick to Emeka. Now that I think of it, I don't know if it was really love anymore or just my nature to be loyal.

Ebuka was not as handsome as Emeka, but had more and great potentials. He was grounded, made dreams and followed through. He has met with my family and bonded greatly with them.

Emeka never asked after my family. He never for once mentioned that I should say hello to my mother in his letters. It disturbed me a bit, knowing I am a senior daughter and carry enormous responsibility on my shoulders.

After the time we met, and the two weeks we spent in the village, I had not seen Emeka one on one again. Wherever he is, he is now twenty one – a man. I wondered how he is, what he will be doing at what ever hour, I was thinking of him. His letters stopped coming as they used to, from weekly to monthly. It has for the past two years graduated to quarterly. Still I waited patiently.

Ebuka sent me emails through my younger ones, through his family and my neighbors. Anyone who goes to cybercafé must return with a mail for me. I got to read at least three mails from Ebuka every week, in just three weeks that he left.

Valentine's Day evening, I was strolling out to get an ice-cream to eat some of the cookies Ebuka sent me from London. All of a sudden, I was hugged and lifted up from behind by a very tall man. Who could this be? I turned around and was so glad that it turned out to be Emeka. He was so handsome, he took my breath away. He smelled very expensive, looked so sexy, something in the inside of me tingled.

Everyone at the supermarket watched as he lifted me again and turned me around, both of us laughing. My prince is here, nothing else mattered. My parents were out of town and my siblings were visiting an aunt. I was home alone. It was perfect.

We bought my ice-cream- I paid and we went home. When we got home we sat down and ate all the goodies Ebuka sent me. Meanwhile lover boy came to see me after four years on Valentine's Day for that matter and I was quite concerned that he came empty handed.

I quickly told him about Ebuka, and explained my position but oddly he kept quiet, saying nothing. But I could notice him staring lustfully at me. He didn't hide it because he touch me at private places and teased me about being his wife.

He didn't say much about aviation school, in his letters. Just a few words saying he is fine and telling me his missed me.

I asked about everyone, school, health, he ignored my questions and spoke about parties, parties and parties! About young guys making it fraudulently and acquiring properties in the capital cities.

Night fall came and he had his bath and waited for me in bed (my bed) while I cleaned up. He touched nothing while I did all the chores. I thought about telling him to come assist me but decided against it.

That night Emeka deflowered me. I refused to believe that was his first time too. It couldn't be. The patient way he handled himself during foreplay which lasted for over an hour. I thought I would die. He kissed me everywhere, licked everywhere and when it seemed like I am going to get to climax, he would pause and begin all over again. Thank God for the small transistor radio in the room. The whole neighborhood would have heard me –the one and only, miss goody-two shoes moan aloud without a care in the world from sexual ecstasy. I never knew that would be the only night of passion with Emeka. By the time he deflowered me, I was sure I would have raped him if he waited any longer.

It was a new journey for me. I was a woman. He stayed the next night too. I noticed He had only one priority; to look good. He bathes and dresses up and that's it. I did all the chores and cooked. He asked me for money so he could go into town. When I frowned, he quickly added that it was a loan he would pay back, so I gave him.

Later that night, he returned home very late and drunk. I was shocked. He dragged me to himself as soon as I locked the door. He tore my night dress off my body, threw me to the floor and raped me in the cruelest ways possible right there in my father's parlor. It went on forever. He lasted for close to an hour. He was very rough and when I tried to stop him he slapped me and held me by my throat. He was too strong for me. I begged him and reminded him that I am his wife to be and he needed not treat me like a prostitute. He got pissed off and slapped me harder telling me all women are the same. If I was a car, the best term to use to describe my state was been 'vandalized'!

Then he stopped, and the next thing I saw was very smelling vomit all over my face. I didn't see it coming because my eyes were shut very tight. He fell on me and slept off snoring almost immediately.

I laid there for what seemed like eternity, bathed in stench. I pushed him off me and ran to the bathroom to clean up. There I cried like I would die. I have never in my life, been treated so disgustingly by anyone. I guess the high protective hedge built around me with so much love has been penetrated with such deep darkness. I would never remain the same again.

After what seemed like forever, I returned to clean up the sitting room. Out of spite, I left him there and slept on the couch till morning. I refused to let what happened sink in. No, this could not have happened. While I tried to sleep, sleep refused to come. I was reliving the trauma, it kept replaying again and again in my head without my consent. I jumped up and rush to the mirror. My cheeks were bruised, neck bruised and also one of my eyes, my right eye was swollen and almost closed. I ached all over. Down there I felt so sore. I took pain killers and waited.

He woke up and asked for pain killers. I got up still pretty much shaken and in fear ran to the kitchen and returned with two tablets and gave him. He drank it and asked why he was lying on the floor of the sitting room and not the bedroom. I kept quiet. Imagine the selfishness? He thinks only about himself. He got up and went in to clean himself up. Slowly moving about like a robot. Not asking what went down. He couldn't move his head.

He came out all clean, looking very weak and it was then he realized I was injured. He asked me if he did that to me. I started crying, wondering how all this could be possible. He fell on his knees and began to beg. He cried even more than I did. And anytime he noticed any new spot on me, he would resume crying. He pleaded with me and told me it's a one time thing that he would never lay a finger on me anymore.

Few hours later after breakfast (I had to cook in my condition), he told me there was someone at the door. I went and it was a neighbor with a mail from Ebuka. He printed the pictures, Ebuka sent along with the mail. Emeka saw the mail and all the intimidating pictures of Ebuka and hell was let loose.

I was interrogated like a common criminal. Emeka was the accuser, the judge and the jury. I was found guilty of all the chargers and he demanded that I should never contact Ebuka or have anything to do with him with effect from that second he was speaking. He reminded me that we took an oath to be together for life and I should respect that. He then went on to shamelessly ask me to give him transport fare back home. I just went in, got the cash he required- God knows I was eager to see him leave. He collected the cash and left, promising to contact me.

That was the beginning of Emeka's reign of terror in my life. I can't put to words how many other beatings and rape I suffered in the hands of Emeka. There were death threats but I tried to stay focused.

Months flew into years, I went through school, secretly speaking to Ebuka, who still continued professing his love for me. He returned to Nigeria and resumed with a top oil and gas company, where he was doing very well. He was my support system.

I realized Emeka lacked Focus. He couldn't put himself together to round up one thing. He dropped out of one academic program to another. He never told me what happened to his aviation school education. He lies to his parents and blackmails his sisters for money. His mother could never see anything wrong with him. She answered to his every wimp.

When he finally took me home to meet his family, they where overjoyed that such a beautiful, calm and put together damsel has agreed to marry their son. They danced for joy. The mother wouldn't let go of my arm. She took me everywhere with her. Their joy was so over the top that I became suspicious but naïvely tagged along.

My heart was now with Ebuka. I was very much in love with him but fear couldn't make me do otherwise. I tried to make Emeka get tired of me. I refused to do stuff for him but he kept manipulating me to answer to his every demand. But now lying here at my death bed, I finally knew the truth- I just realized now that I was WEAK. With my personality type there was no way I could ever have broken free of Emeka. I didn't have that courage, the determination or self will to fight.

We finally got married! Yes, we got married. The parents and sisters went all the way out to give us a fabulous wedding. I was there in person but not in spirit. I tried to hide my pain and my disgust by putting up a smiling face. But inside of me I cried for Ebuka. I loved him so much and wanted badly to be his wife. But my mind kept taking me back to the oath we took in the village years back and I resigned to fate.

Emeka was jobless. No university education. No skill whatsoever. He lived at his parent's house all his life, been fed and taken care of by them. They got him a flat when we got married and furnished it for us. I don't know how, but I just tagged along.

It was when I got married, I knew there where two kinds of water on earth. One, water and the other blood. I saw hell; I was violated on a daily basis. He asked me to do odd sexual rituals. Once he came home with a cucumber and wanted to explore. He desired anal sex, and when I resisted, he beat me blue black. Despite all this I couldn't find any strength to move on. I couldn't even say or bring up the topic of the blood oath. Emeka owned me and he reminds me daily.

My eyes were opened the day I caught him cheating. I laughed so hard that I lost my balance and broke a tooth. So Emeka could cheat? Then the gods had to be my side then. The only thing that had made me endure this marriage was the oath we swore before the gods. And it's not a hidden fact that the gods can be merciless. I knew no one forced me so I had been taking in everything calmly because I knew I ignorantly got myself into this. Now the threat is no longer there (as I had assumed), I am free-I reasoned!

I moved out that same night without thinking twice.

My parents wasted no time in returning my dowry. Emeka kept threatening me but I refused to be moved by him. He repeatedly told me that my life is in his hands- I never understood what he meant until now. One day he attacked me. I didn't know where I got the strength from but I got some thugs and they beat Emeka until he swore never to come near me again.

Mission accomplished. I moved on with life. I hid my pain very well. I was seen as the beauty queen without anyone knowing the battles I was fighting; no one knew the tears hidden beneath the smile.

Emeka and I had only traditional marriage. He has this belief that women should not be married in court, that women are deceitful. If only he knew. What a relief.

After two years of my separation from Emeka, Ebuka and I got married. We were together enjoying marital bliss for eleven months until disaster struck. For no reason, Ebuka began acting strange. He started staying away from me and stopped picking my calls and called only when he felt like. I was pregnant at the time. He eventually stopped calling and coming home altogether. Efforts by everyone to get Ebuka to at least say what the problem was, wasn't effective.

Due to stress, I developed high blood pressure and wit it came pre-eclampsia. I was lucky to escape with my life but lost the baby. That sealed the deed. Ebuka's parents came one day, very sad and confused and asked that my family seat and discuss dissolution of marriage. Their Son has sent them to dissolve the marriage. I thought I would die from heartbreak.

It took almost a year to completely dissolve our marriage. It was so surprising how Ebuka moved on fast. He got married almost immediately after our divorce and relocated out of Nigeria.

I still can't put my misery into words. Ebuka was the best thing that happened to me in my life. To live without him was like asking a fish to live without water. My life was aimless and lacked purpose. I had no reason to wake up in the mornings. I had nothing to look forward to every bright new day. I cursed my life. I hated my destiny. Who would have known? Who would have guessed that that bright and beautiful young lady would end up with a destiny as dark as mine? There was no future for me. No baby even to console me of my miserable life. I was alone, yes surrounded by people but all alone.

I became chronically depressed and began to fall sick often. I fell sick every now and then. I became a shadow of me. Separation from Ebuka was the most difficult chapter of my life. I loved him more than my own life and I knew he felt same. I have grown used to him been by my side through every difficult issues of my life.

After Ebuka, no man wanted to date me. I became a one night stand to men and they all left after that night. They never picked my calls after that one night. Many false prophets diagnosed my issues as disturbance from the marine kingdom. They said my spirit husband in the spirit world is the one responsible for my failed relationships.

My parents spent money trying to fight off this so called wicked spirit. Things did not change instead they turned for the worst. I could not understand.

Two years back, the sickness struck in full. I was positive to every ailment on earth, asides HIV and TB. I was labeled an HIV patient but I wasn't. Funny enough, despite the fact that my system was failing, my results came back negative to HIV and tuberculosis.

Few weeks back, my grandma took the traditional route and we were told to look for Emeka. The answer lies with him. We finally located him. And he told me proudly that the day of the oath taking he didn't lick my blood, that it was a one way thing. So whatever I am suffering is a result of the oath I took.

We went back to the traditionalist and he told us bring Emeka to the shrine since he alone can set me free from the oath before I could begin to heal. All search for Emeka has proved abortive. Till date, no one knows where Emeka is. It's like he fell off the face off the earth.

As I speak, my skin is falling off. I no longer eat pepper. Any food given to me, have to be over-cooked to remove the taste.

I smell so bad even I can't stand my stench. I urinate and excrete on my body. My mum has started wearing me diapers.

I am finally home to die and I can't wait to. I need peace. The pain I pass through on a daily basis is unbearable. I just wanted to tell my story. I believe that one or two persons may learn from it. I know that my story though strange as it sounds is been practiced everyday by naïve young people. My story could save a life.

Nnenna passed on a few weeks later. She passed through hell the last week of her life; it was terrible. First she went blind, then maggot began to crawl out from all openings in her body. Her nose, ears, mouth, anus and vagina. They came out in the evenings and all through the night. In the morning, we would find her covered in multitude of maggots. It was as if her insides where decomposing while she was alive. She would scream all night long crying from the pains she is passing through. She begged us to kill her and save her the unbearable anguish. My brothers came at the final hours and the doctor tried to give her very strong sedatives and pain killers but it was not effective. Sleep could not be induced. This was strictly a spiritual matter. In the eyes of the gods, she has broken the law and they are killing her very slowly and mercilessly for it. We all begged for death to come quick for she daily begged us to have mercy and kill her.

One cold night when she stopped screaming, we knew it was over.

The story of Nnenna ended that day. Nnenna the beautiful damsel, our beauty queen, has passed on. All her dreams and bright future cut off shortly due to an oath she ignorantly took.

Nothing can ever heal the pain forever engrained in our hearts. And I will make it my lives goal to educate young ladies, especially those in the secondary school against such dastardly act. If a man cannot love you without taking an oath, then the relationship should never be. Nothing good will ever come from it. Nothing! It can only lead to death.

STORY 10

Faiza's Story

I got into the front seat of our husbands car and slowly sat down. I took quick glances, here and there trying to see if anyone was watching me. No one in sight. Good! I slowly adjusted my body on the car seat. The seat is so hard, no single comfort whatsoever. It made the pain so unbearable. Finally I was able to position myself comfortably. Breathing a sigh of relief, I was thankful that I would be driven to school and wouldn't have to walk all three kilometers. Today was not going to be a good day. I knew the signs. My body could tell the difference. Some days were worse than the others. None was good or better. Every day, a living hell. I pinched my thighs, remembering that was how my mum taught me to snap out of self pity. She told me, I had started on a very tedious journey. Its one journey that needs strength not stress. I need to be in charge of my self to face the turbulent years that lies ahead. And she stressed that if I try to be relaxed I would fare better because been scared makes the pain overrated.

Maigida {Trans: head of the house; also means husband} came out and got into the car. Talatu who had been standing outside pretending to be busy, so as not to get into the car with me alone, finally raised her head up and walked to the back door, opened and got in. Talatu is my husband's second wife.

I watched the beautiful landscape as the car drove by. I loved nature. I was in awe of everything created by the Almighty God- The trees, the flowers, the insects etc. I spent my younger years playing about with my siblings with and around everything nature. I know that one day, I will love to study something that relates to nature. And I am positive that I would excel.

"Oooouch!!!" I screamed

"Me ya faru?" {Trans: What is the matter?} Our husband enquired from me.

"Ba Komi ba." {Trans: It's nothing!} I answered.

The agonizing pain, from down below my abdomen, reminded me of my 'predicament' (oh! My mother would kill me for referring to my current situation as one)

And oh! So Sorry!! My bad. Let me introduce myself; my name is Fa'iza! (Pronounced Fah Ezar!) I'm thirteen years old, in Junior Secondary two and am a woman.

Yes! The third wife of my husband. My marriage is just three months old. And yes, I perform my conjugal duties. Am been "serviced" regularly as a new bride. I was told the pain comes with the territory and would subside with time.

I am a petite young woman, who is pretty inquisitive and full of life. I am currently been driven to school in our husbands rickety 505 Salon Car. Seated arm-crossed behind me at the back seat is Talatu, my mate who's sixteen and in Junior Secondary three. She's had two kids and the third child is on his/her way. I don't see her leaving the junior secondary just yet. She's going to have her hands full with two toddlers and a new baby.

Zainab the eldest wife is twenty one now and is in Senior Secondary One. She's had five kids. Today like the past two weeks, Zainab will be walking to school- yes the whole three kilometers. That's after dropping all her kids in School. Her last child just over a year old, she drops off with her mother.

Maigida insists that Education is the key. He demands that all his wives and kids attend school without fail. In as much as they all grumbled, they knew they couldn't go against the law of the head of the family. This I am sure is the main reason, why my Papa married me off to him. Papa is so fond of me. He knows I love books and nature and I love life.

He promised me that he will get me a man who would take care of my education. That would be one of the conditions of my marriage. And it panned out exactly as my Papa desired. Papa did the much he could on my dowry; He provided my bed, table, room divider- All the furniture I needed. Mama and Grandma from my papa's side bought me all my kitchen utensils. My elder brother gave a compact disc set, so I can listen to CDs on different issues. Papa buys me CD's whenever he goes to town.

I moved into my husband's home well provided for and this made everyone in my new home hold me in high esteem. I had all the latest furniture's, electronic gadgets and all. Both wives envied me- oh yes, I know when I am envied (*giggling*). As I go about in my colorful wrappers, I see them watch secretly with eyes filled with envy. When I open my apartment door when it's hot, I see them sneak a quick peak. And I don't mind. I am a free person. But Grandma told me to be cautious. But I have often wondered, what could be more hurting and dangerous than what my husband do to me at night when he comes in to me.

I pinched myself again – refusing to get into a depressive mood. Ma and Grandma have all gone through the same process and I must be strong to go through it too. If they can, I definitely will.

I made a mental check to see if I took my drugs. Yes, I did! My mama secretly gave me family planning bills as I left home. She promised to supply them regularly without fail. I am not sure this goes down well with our religion but Mama says my future is more important to her than any religious law she has promised that she will assist me in fulfilling my dreams of becoming a graduate. She says I must become someone and fight to stop this. If it can't be eradicated, then the conditions should be altered.

My family suffered a great loss the previous year. I lost my beautiful elegant senior sister. She died through child birth. I can still remember the day clearly. It was a black Thursday for our family. Neetu as we fondly called her has returned to my mum to have her baby. She was in such terrible pain. I remember thinking how awful it is that she had to be in pains on her birthday, when she should be eating sweets and cake. But her baby insisted on being born that day. Neetu died shortly after her baby girl was born. She died on her birthday, and without seeing her baby.

I had stubbornly refused to leave the room (which was in fact a store room for maize and rice) when she was in labor. I stood there and witnessed the birth of my niece. I have never ever seen so much blood in my life. Somehow I knew this could not be right and I had the premonition that disaster was knocking. I watched keenly. When the baby's head was crowning, l was sure I would pass out. But strangely I didn't. Probably because curiosity took over the better part of me. I watched as they cleaned her up with wrappers. They kept changing one soaked wrapper after another till she passed out. Neetu never woke up from that sleep. It's so painful. Now my heart is shaken. And I feel deep pain in my soul and in my body.

I turned to look at my husband in the driver's seat, driving so calmly. He turned and looked at me with lustful eyes- Yes now, Lustful really! Like he does, when he comes in my apartment to perform conjugal duties. I noticed He relates with me in a different way. He has read many books. He knows about a lot of stuff too and has loads of answers to my questions. He is my friend. He's by far smarter than me and I know He manipulates me sometimes. Like on my wedding night, he tricked me. He told me that we are about to become man and wife. And he explained patiently in details what he was about to do. He then ticked me off by telling me there's something loads of women didn't know. That he would tell me the secret. I asked what? He said a woman releases same liquid that men have too before ejaculation. But he said few women don't know this because they never get to see it or experience orgasm.

He asked if I was ready to see it. I quickly relaxed myself, waiting to experience and see this hidden secret. As you know I never got to see it that night or any night till now. He still keeps insisting that one day when I have learnt to relax and go with the flow, I would see it. How can I relax with that huge uncircumcised something standing and probing at me? The thought set my stomach on a tumble. Everything in there twisted and turned. That's my large intestines am sure.

My husband is an intimidating six feet and four inches tall, weighing one hundred and eighty kilograms. He is soft spoken and kind. He is forty three. There are so many things I don't understand about my new family. So many questions I'd love to ask. I don't know much, but common sense has made me keep my mouth shut and watch.

My husband took a turn into a petrol station to get petrol. I got down to take a break from the car, and stretch my legs. As I turned, I bumped into a young woman, probably in her early twenties. I was greeted by a familiar stench- the annoying smell of urine. I knew immediately what the poor young lady was suffering from. My heart sank. I looked into her eyes and saw strength. Strong will and strength. 'The common trait of our women'. I gave her an encouraging smile, which was returned shyly. My mind began to wander quickly. I looked again at the young woman, trying to determine her status and read more from her outlook. She looked un-kept but by far neater that what I see everyday. She looked cared for. Maybe if she had on her a deodorant or body spray it could have helped hide the smell. Even a good soap to cleanse. But we are in a faraway village, deep down in the heart of Kaduna State. A little bit away from modestly urban area. I always laugh about the name of my village, which ironically means "town of mediocre". How cliché! And to think that those of us living here in town are not up to thirty percent of our town's population. The remaining members of my clan have refused to come to town to enjoy the little development we enjoy. We get to enjoy power supply regularly because we are a small community. We don't have too many electronic gadgets and appliances at home. Not many of us can afford fridges, television set etc. so the power consumption is pretty low thus constant electric supply.

Our small community doesn't grow that much; I don't know the precise number. We only get to see new recruits of corps member every other year. We have a small bakery. There is presently no telecommunication but cables are been put in place. We are told before the year runs out that would be connected to the world. That's something I look forward to seriously. We have just two churches and a mosque. We have a very massive hospital that to me is the beauty of this small town. We have just one petrol station. There's a lodge, I see on my way to school. Don't know if it's functional. But most importantly, we have a Federal Government Girls College – which to me is FATE telling me I am blessed and highly favored.

Fuel bought, we both got into the car. The three kilometer journey, takes ages because of the rough and bad spot all over the road. We have to drive at snail speed; also my very pregnant mate behind at the back seat is another reason to drive slowly. Our considerate husband wouldn't want her hurt. As we pulled out, the young lady smiled and waved at me. I waved back. Having a car here is classy. Every one respects you when you are driven about in one. It doesn't matter if it's a dilapidated old Peugeot 505. Where there are blind people, the one eyed man is the king, right?

"She has VVF" I told my husband as he drove off. "I can't understand it! How does it get this bad?

My husband simply grunted, but said nothing. He doesn't talk much when we have company. But when we are together in private, he opens up and we discuss a lot. I think He doesn't talk much to me openly outside in order to protect me from jealousy and also to firmly control his household. He doesn't want to be seen as one that's partial.

My mind went to my own mother who has suffered from it from as long as I can remember. Vestico Vagina Fistula (VVF) is an epidemic. In my village, one out of five ladies suffers from VVF. When you visit the hospital it's a sorry sight.

Vestico Vagina Fistula is our curse. Due to early marriage, most of us always end up pregnant before the age of fifteen. Those who get pregnant earlier even give birth at age twelve. I know firsthand young women that are my juniors that are mothers. And being married to older uncircumcised men (I keep saying uncircumcised because in my mind's eye, I remember seeing Christian boys at hospital with shorter penises than my own brothers at home.) who in my opinion destroys firsthand the elastic nature of the vagina. We hear it's not only in this northern part of Nigeria but even girls my age in the south suffer this. Some not even up to eleven years old, are given out in marriage.

Just the night before, news had reached us about my mum in pain. And it was a subject we discussed while in bed. My well read (well read in my opinion) husband told me he has read quite a lot about it and witnessed more than a few. He told me a dreadful story he said he read online while in Kaduna.

I was particularly interested in this topic because even I stand a risk of contracting it. He began by breaking it down for me to understand in a lame way.

"Vestico Vagina Fistula (VVF)

Loads of young girls like me that are usually between the ages of eleven-fifteen years of age, get married early like I am now.

These girls become pregnant almost immediately after marriage and go on to have babies at this tender age. Their pelvic which is predominately very tight becomes a big issue when it comes to labor because the whole experience is rigorous and the baby's head can't pass through to be delivered. When this happens, which is usually in local and under-developed areas, the traditional mid-wife most times result to assisting the young mother by creating a tear in the vagina with the intention of making an elaborate passage way for the easy and safe delivery of the baby. And this is usually where the problem 'Vestico vagina fistula' is born. Due to the tear, she's now left with a leakage and the new mother experiences a situation where urine and excreta passes through her vagina, instead of the natural passage way meant for them. It is so heart breaking to see women suffers this. My mum suffers from it. And she's just twenty nine years old.

Our Grandma (my mum's mother) told of a real life story that happened at Ikot Ekpere, in Akwa Ibom State, southern part of Nigeria.

This young lady was also between the eleven-fifteen age group. Now I don't know if she was married or what the circumstances that led to her been pregnant but the story centers on her pregnancy.

She was said to have not registered for ante-natal care and when she was due, she suffered a two week long labor during which she was shuttled from one traditional mid-wife to another. With that not producing any positive results, they switched from one Church to the next. After two weeks of hell, they finally retorted to a mediocre means.

This may sound too difficult or even impossible to believe but my Grandma swears it happened. A long stick they said was passed through her mouth to her abdomen (Africa!!!) and used to push down the uterus. And lo, what came out forcefully was a dead decomposed baby. The young mother (can I call her that? Since she lost her baby) had multiple internal ruptures and had to undergo twenty different surgical operations in a short four year span. She also had to be rehabilitated.

My dear hubby Bala also said he came across an eye opening read. He got the information from an abstract written by Fafoyin A. He didn't say who Fafoyin was, if he is a professor or a medical practitioner or a journalist. I guess when I have access to the internet I would find out. But the story my grandma told us, he said Fayoyin also collaborated it. So that makes it true then? I think so!

Bala dear also told me of another case also discussed in the abstract. He said in down south Nigeria, Same Ikot Ekpere – Akwa Ibom State, a 21 year old graduating university student studying arts, who this time around has faithfully attended her ante-natal clinic for 38 weeks (just two weeks to go!) during her pregnancy suddenly stopped. She stopped attending ante- natal of such an important and critical period because she got a prophecy in her church that her labor would be difficult and complicated and lead to her death, after she would have gone through caesarean operation to deliver her baby. So she opted to stay home.

She finally went into labor, and the gruesome labor pain lasted for seventy two hours and led to the delivery of a dead baby. After that, she began hemorrhaging seriously. And whoever the birth attendants were (local Birth attendant or Church members), they could not assist in removing her placenta. This made them back go to the hospital where she had refused to continue attending in the first place.

During the process of expelling her placenta, it was discovered that she had developed VVF. But this young lady still insisted on being discharged before the repair operation could be done on her, arguing that whatever her condition was, her health would be restored in Church.

She left and after three months when the expected healing did not take place, she returned again to the hospital for solution. After examination, she was discovered to be pregnant again!! (Having sex until that condition? Lord have mercy!) The second fetus was born through C.S, and then died later due to the entire inexperienced disturbance to her pregnancy.

Religion has become an issue to women in our country. Religious leaders play on the intelligence of their members and make them take unhealthy decisions. Well that's a topic for another day.

My mum takes care of herself very well. I don't know the details about her challenge with VVF. But I know she's determined not to let me have that awful experience. My grandmother and my mum are monitoring me from a distance. They pressured my dad into getting me a man that would suit me and understand my dreams. And father did a good job.

In my family, they look to me to bring them out of the hole they have found themselves and I intend not to fail them. My husband has seen the ambitious part of me and he is excited about the challenge. He was cautioned about my well being and he has promised not to be hard on me.

Asides the difficult nights of pain and discomfort and the mornings that follows, I am grateful. Am grateful because I know that life has dealt me a better deal. First I came to life through a mother that though culture has taught her to be silent and not be heard, she has secretly in her heart nurtured me to one day be an advocate of change.

Grandma's on both sides of my family dot on me. That again, is another awesome blessing. While I was growing up and still lived with my parents, I remember waking up to daily praises from both of them. As I go about, they sing me songs of praise. Makings up stories, how like queen Amina of Zaria I would change the lives of our women for the better. They sing and compare me to Mary Slessor, who stopped the killing of twins. Every single waking day of my life before I got married, I woke up to praises. I had other names from my local dialect. The names are all prayers. They use my names to make a song. And they sing and dance. When I sit, to make my hair. From start to finish both my grandmothers would sing, dance and gesticulate and beg God to add extra years to their life and good eye sight so that they can witness my rise to glory. They created musical instrument from beverage cans and would use cutleries to drum on the empty cans and make me beautiful music. I have enough self-confidence to go around 1 million young ladies my age and more. My self-esteem is over the sky and I feel no fear. I am psychologically, emotionally and mentally balanced. I never feel intimidated. In fact my biggest challenge is learning to control my mouth. My grandmother's love made me so.

My father had often watched and encouraged them, with a smiling face.

Am grateful to God, for my father also. He choose the best husband available for me. A man who understands the purpose of my life and goes the extra mile to give the needed education. He always drives me to school. Helps me with my homework when he has the chance. And he prints out articles from the Internet when he travels to towns that have internet facilities and also buys me current affairs magazines.

I have so much to be thankful for. I am not looking to have any children till am through University, which my Grandma, Mum and I have calculated to be nine years tops. So I am facing my studies so seriously because I know I have to accomplish much, in the time ahead.

I see so much pain around me. There's so much suffering. Women need to be educated on how to empower themselves and make their lives more useful. They need to be informed on issues about their well being. Too much ignorance revolving all about us.

In my school, there are sick cases of young girls who need psychologists, therapist etc. So many of them are traumatized. So many of them are so dirty and unkempt. Some get pregnant back to back, year after year.

There's a silent trend going on here that the rest of the world is ignorant of. The rate with which these young women are used and dumped with no one to care for their young bodies and babies is astonishing. You see a young girl of sixteen looking worn out. It's like she's faded. Having three children and on top of that she's divorced. Divorce is rampant here. Loads of young girls are thrown out of marriage daily to create space for new younger virgins. These girls, still in their teens are left to cater for their children and themselves. With little or no help from anyone.

It easy to see one girl in every ten divorced. Right here in northern Nigeria. And we scream like the Westerners are doing something strange when under our noses young teenagers are made wives and raped continuously and carelessly under the umbrella of marriage. Are these not Pedophiles?

Young mothers are abandoned by their husbands emotionally, physically and financially. Often they dump them to cater for their kids alone while these men hop to look for the next available virgins to exploit.

These should stop! It would take time. That I am certain of. But time is all we have. I will cry out when due and tell the world that in the midst of this madness, I rose stronger with support of family and became someone. People, parents and husbands should do same. These girls have dreams too...yes, I believe they do.

"Fa'iza!!! Fa'iza!!!" Bala's Voice brought me back to the present.

"Muna nan" {Trans: We are here}

"Na geni" {Trans: I see} I said and opened the door to go out. He held my hand, then quickly withdrew it. I paused. And we waited for my mate at the back seat to get out.

As she thanked him and proceeded to walk away, He brought out his other arm and stretched both towards me. He gave me a warm hug. I felt safe, secure and much loved. He then stretched his hands to me, I held both. I am fond of this man. I have to be Sincere. But am just thirteen, what do I know really? He makes me feel special! I have my father to be thankful for and life has been so faithful to me. I know it's for a divine reason.

"Maraba Zuwa Makaranta" (Trans: Welcome to School.) My darling Bala said "Fatan alheri zuwa ga masuyina" (Trans: Have a great day, my love)

To which, I replied "Nagode So sei" {thank you so much}

"Allah taimake ki yau" (Trans: God bless your day) he said and kissed both hands.

Joy filled my spirit. Imagine your husband blessing you every single morning just as you begin your day. Despite the pains from last nights love making, my soul is at peace. I feel so lucky and am grateful to Allah for his mercies. As I walked through the school gate, I heard Bala's car horn, I turned and watched him. He waved and threw me a kiss then drove off. He would be here to pick me up, like he always does.

I walked towards my classroom, smiling; this is where the molding begins.

I looked to the sky and said a silent thank you once again to the Almighty God, then happily walked into my classroom with determination and commitment, knowing that my tomorrow is going to be GREAT!!!

FAIZA

STORY 11

Katie's Story

I stood fixated to a spot lost in thoughts, then slowly began walking around my baby's nursery. As I paced about, I checked all the wonderful and lovely baby items we had bought with so much love and joyful anticipation. Some baby items as old as ten years. I picked up a small teddy bear and slowly sat on the rocking chair.

I always come here to relax. Sitting down here soothes me. I have been having series of nightmares, going back few weeks. I don't know if it's proper to refer to it as nightmares because all I see are my dead children. And if I have to believe what my relatives are saying of late then I have been seeing my dead 'child' in my dreams.

I have no more tears to shed. It's pure miracle that I have not developed high blood pressure. All my body has passed through these ten years is enough to drain me psychologically, emotionally and especially physically. But I have decided for a long while now to be bigger than my challenges. It's not what people say about me that count, but what I tell myself. And I believe that I am going to be a mother of a living child soon. Nothing can break me.

A tingling pain at my lower back bone came on quickly and left. "IT'S TIME!!!" I quickly picked up my phone and dialed Kayode's (my hubby) number. Kayode is the one true blessing of my life. The only one who has shared my pain and made me feel secured. He has made sure I realize that I am not alone on this journey.

He picked up call and I told him that it's time! He told me he would be home in a jiffy. I tried standing up but my very pregnant body was too much for my legs to carry. I decided to sit back and wait for my dear hubby. He has packed up all my ante-natal/ delivery needs, all ready in my suitcase since the first day I entered my due date. It's going to be a while before I experience another contraction. So I just stayed put and tried to relax and not fret.

I sat back and before I knew, I dozed off.

It was the same dream…

I saw myself pregnant, then in labor then I give birth to this beautiful baby. The most beautiful baby I have ever seen. And I guess the same is true for the nurses and doctors present. For they were all wowed just like I was sight of the baby. She was very fair and with dark hair.

While we were all happy and smiling and chatting right there in the delivery room, she began to turn blue right before our eyes. Without wasting much time she passed on.

All efforts to bring her back proved abortive. She was gone. I was inconsolable. My hubby and I wept bitterly.

I saw myself being discharged and going home empty handed-still crying.

Then I was back at the delivery room once again. I saw myself in labor, then delivery. And again the same beautiful baby girl. Then after all the hoos and haas! She passed on. Then all the crying that leads to me being discharged and sent home.

Then I see myself being pregnant the third time. Then labor and delivery. But this time, no death at the delivery room. We happily took her home and rejoiced. We were so happy to have taken delivery of this perfect looking Angel. But our joy was short lived, as she died in her sleep the evening she was named. She cried all through her naming ceremony as if not happy with the name we have given her. Then another episode of crying ensued. The corpse was taken from me forcefully and taken to an unknown place to bury.

Then I was pregnant again and again in labor, then delivery. This time a different hospital and the nurses were screaming with delight to see such a lovely perfect baby but I kept quite. Knowing fully well the calamity that may befall me. And true to my fears the morning after her naming she passed on. I had little tears to shed.

"Then I was pregnant again..."

"But the sharp pain from my lower back brought me back to reality. I was in no doubt that I am in the early stage of labor. After the painful contraction stopped, I tried to stand up. As I did, I made a mental note to check the timing of next contraction. I walked to the window and checked to see if my hubby was approaching. He was not. So I called again and he begged that he was held in traffic. I moved around a bit. There was nothing for me to do. Everything was ready.

Sitting down once again, my mind went back to the dream. Yes, it was a dream, a nightmare but it was in fact my reality. It all happened life to me. Every detail of that the dream my hubby and I has re-lived in reality.

My name is Abosede and I have been married for ten years.

As I said earlier, the nightmares I had recently been experiencing are my real life experiences. I have been pregnant five (5) consecutive times, and I lost the babies all five times. After the fourth pregnancy, my hubby and I decided to do some research.

And our research landed us on the strangest of stories and myth. The Abiku/Ogbanje myth.

I need to point out that before this time we have had countless encounters with false prophets that bleed us dry financially. They kept asking us for ridiculous amounts of money. Over the years, especially during the four years of the first two pregnancy and the first trimester of the third, we spent over five million naira. We were down on all of our savings. We were asked to sell our cherished and priced properties. This we did. Both our luxury cars went one after the other. Followed by our expensive jewelries, even I had to let go of my diamond encrusted wedding band and get a cheaper one. One pastor asked me to take my box of Hollandaise (A wrapper of pride, and owned by only the rich in southern Nigeria). I had about fifty pieces of Hollandaise priced at eighteen thousand naira per piece, when you multiply that by fifty, you get more than half a million naira (Three thousand dollar). But the pastor instructed that I sell to the first person who stepped forward to bargain with me. I was not to negotiate whatever, but to sell at the first priced offered. On getting to the market, I still can't fathom how it all happened but the pastor's wife ironically appeared before me and named a heartbreaking price. She said she would pay twenty thousand naira (just a little over ten dollars) for a box of wrapper that should cost nothing less than three hundred thousand naira going by cargo (naija slang for "used goods") value. Alarms went off in my head but I timidly accepted the twenty thousand naira and watch her ask her aids to lift my box of precious wrappers and carried off to her car. Those wrappers were precious to me. Some were handed down to me from my great grand mother. Some were bought by my husband as my dowry demanded. Some were gifts from my parents before my wedding. Now I was left with nothing. I couldn't connect the sales of my wrapper to stopping the death of my newborn babies. But when one is desperate, he/she is eager to follow any path that may lead to solution to his/her problems. If my present pregnancy would lead me to keeping my baby, I wouldn't worry about fifty pieces of wrapper. But we still lost the babies.

Secretly following a close relative to a Babalawo (Voodoo doctor) we encountered more issues. The pastors all claimed that our problem was spiritual. Some said I had spirit husband and some said it was my hubby's wicked spirit wife. Others blamed either my mother or my mother-in-law and some said it was my husband's ex-girlfriends.

Now the Babalawo brought into light another world of issues. The first claimed that, my husband's past life is what is disturbing us. That my hubby used to be a very wicked king. And killed a lot of women, after raping them. He was so violent. But when he reincarnated, He returned as a peace loving man. But his peace was not to be, because the women he cheated on and treated badly in his past life are responsible for the death of his children. We were asked to get the heart of a live lion, while it's still warm and red.

Another asked us to get the nails of an alligator. We were asked to pay ridiculous amounts of money to get someone willing to get these items for us. One asked us to buy twenty one candles, each twenty-one thousand naira (about one hundred and twenty dollar per candle). Another half a million gone. We did all we were asked because we had no idea where our salvation would come from.

We ended up with four dead babies and when the fifth was on the way, someone approached my mother and my mother-in-law.

That was how we got to know about ABIKU. We were told this could be our position. In fact my mother in law was sure that this was the problem.

Abiku/ogbanje are spirit beings that are believe to enter the womb of pregnant women and take over the fetus. They live from life to life and do not have the luxury of mortality. The peace of death, which mortals enjoy is something alienated to them. They roam from life after life. They sell the tears of the aggrieved as money in the spirit world for a very expensive fee. The sorrow of the aggrieved family is translated to wealth/Power in the spirit world. So they aim to taunt the targeted family and get them to weep as long as possible. That is why they prefer to die when the baby is still young and get the family to grieve deeply.

The Abiku's all come with an agreement with Mother Nature to terminate their life here on earth on a specific date. Some even chose their wedding night to die. Just to cause deep grieve.

The Abikus that agree to stay here longer than childhood, usually go for meetings and events with other members all sojourning here on earth. The leave their bodies and transform into whatever form they desire and go out.

Some even leave their mother's side, while breastfeeding at night and transform into the spirit beings and go out. Then they change back into the human form when they return.

Abikus as we were told can be prevented from dying with these three

(i) The name given to them. When named, the pre-informed parents select names that are usually of complaint or spite.

(ii) The celebration of their birth is ignored. Here everyone acts like they don't see them or appreciate them. No signs of joy or happiness is showed. Instead in some cases, curses are rendered on the baby. Some cases, woman gather around the laboring mother has she is about to have the final push. And once d baby is born they scream Thief! Thief!! Thief!!! "Robber of Joy and peace!!!!" "We know your secret" the babies end up not dying and the parents have enough time to terminate his covenant with the spirit world.

(iii) In the case of the third, the parent leave very long mark on the back of the dead children. The corpse is marked at various part of the body. It is believed that the spirit realm does not welcome anyone back with marks on their bodies. So when they die and you mark them. They are driven from the spirit world and they have no choice than to return to this world and stay permanently

I had my fifth child. And we named her Rotimi (Stay with me). Rotimi stayed till she was twelve months old and passed away. She had the best smile. The most beautiful facial features. Every day we spent with her, it was like borrowed time. And boy, did we savor every moment. She passed on early in the morning of her birthday. We had everything ready to paint the neighborhood Red-we left no stone unturned.

We had everything set for a VVIP party. Red carpet, Printed T-Shirts, had all play items like swimming pool, bouncing castles etc. There was more than enough to eat. And then she choose that particular day of Joy to return.

That day, we all refused to cry. I particularly was stunned. And I refuse to shed a tear. My eyes were dry. Everyone was surprised at my composure. I went about like nothing happened.

Later in the day, she was brought back home, confirmed dead. My hubby in rage, went the extra mile. We had agreed to mark her if she died to make her return and stay permanently. But Kayode out of rage, dissected her small body. Head went off, legs and hands followed. We had noticed that same mark with Rotimi from d marks left from the emergency surgery to resuscitate her. So we believed in truth, she was an Abiku. With this awareness, Kayode showed no mercy. Her dissected corpse was packed in box and buried.

The sound of Kayode's car, brought me back from my thoughts.

I have had few more contractions. On our way to the hospital, we decided on having Caesarean section. I thought I could do normal delivery but from the pains I was getting I didn't have much strength left so we decided to have the surgery done to birth them immediately. I forgot to point out the fact that I am caring twins.

We got the Hospital and told the Doctor our desire and I was immediately prep for surgery.

I was delivered of a boy and a girl. And as doubtful as I am of this whole myth, I was shocked to see my daughter scarred. She had marks around her neck. A dark line, around her arms and her upper thighs, where the legs meet the hips. She's fair, but a dark line runs across these parts, just like the seam on a cloth. It's not rough or anything out of the ordinary, it's just a line like a birthmark.

Every time we bath her, I always wonder and it makes me feel funny.

Years later....

It's Funny but it's true. It may sound unbelievable but it's true. This is West Africa and a lot of things may seem strange to others outside this region, but indeed they do happen.

It's my baby's third birthday, and I have just been delivered of another set of twins; two boys. We had their naming already and everything is fine.

I no longer doubt in my heart that my kids are here to stay. Am happy to have them run around and play so innocently and happily. Having another set of twins, has increased my joy to a whole new level.

I don't know what will happen in the future. I don't know if my years of burying my children are behind me.

But one thing I am sure of is my "STRENGTH!" It is indeed true that what does not kill you, makes you strong. I can't say I won't be shaken if any event were to occur but I know for sure our deep ability to endure hardship and pain like it's no big deal.

I look forward to everyday with my four angels. Am finally through with child birth and now savoring the joys of mother hood. Having lost not one or two but five children back to back, my emotional 'shock absorber' is in a pretty good shape. Also these painful experiences has made me appreciate each day we all wake up and go to bed together. I do not take any new day I get to spend with my kids for granted.

It's the product of where I am born into. Despite the ills of the land, I will always be proud of being a Nigerian. Oh yes!

Abosede

STORY 12

Ndudi's Story

In West Africa, there are quite a number of myths. But the facts and realities on ground is usually harder to believe than any myths.

My life is a solid example. Before I go on to explain my stand in this unbelievable tale, let me first narrate the tale surrounding the main character in my story.

In my village, there's a very large tree. Living within this large tree is a large python. The snake has been rumored to live for about four hundred years and counting (I don't know how true that is).

According to old folklore, during the war, the snake was used as a means to predict possible attack on them. Studying the snake has helped them decide endless times without fail when a war is about to break out. They know war is coming to them when the snake begins to swell. And when it returns to its normal size, it indicates that there shall be peace again.

Now this snake is revered amongst the villagers. It is worshipped as a god and the villagers believe in it.

The snake is free to roam the whole village as it pleases. And it is not harmed. But it roams only at night to avoid been attacked by ignorant strangers. It goes about as it desires, into the houses of people. I was told that once, a couple woke up from sleep, only to see the very large snake sleeping between the two of them. They ran out in fear. All effort to move the snake from their matrimonial bed proved abortive, not until its caregiver was summoned.

The caregiver then performs her duties by speaking its language and singing endless praises of the snake. She dances for it and shouts adulations to it. At long last, the snake moved and followed its caregiver ever so slowly towards its residence at the beginning of the village- the very large tree.

The care givers primary life's mission from the day she's chosen is to perform her duties faithfully to the sacred snake. She's to attend to its every need which is a secret from the villagers. Only specific members of the cult can know the rituals to be performed to keep the snake alive. And it has been said to survive century after century.

The caregiver is chosen from a very spiritual process. I don't know how, but when a maiden is chosen, she's not obligated to have an opinion.

In this case, a maiden is a young unmarried woman, usually a virgin. She is never to leave the hut (residence of the caregiver) once chosen. She's free to pick any man she sees fit to be her husband. The man comes in to her and she's not permitted to go to his home to cook, or perform any wifely duty. And most importantly she CANNOT have children; NEVER EVER.

Then also, next in line is she's not permitted to shed tears. She should not dare cry over anything, no matter the weight it carries or how emotionally attached to it she is. For instance, if any of her parents happen to die or even a close friend, she can't shed a single tear, not a drop. If this was to happen, then she dies within twenty-four hours. She's also not permitted to see a corpse. Under no circumstance should she come in contact with a corpse.

And tradition is tradition. She's not permitted to leave the village or travel. From the moment she's chosen, she's to remain in the village till her death. It has been an endless cycle since the beginning of time…. I mean since when the snake was discovered to predict wars.

The last care-giver who is very much in love with her husband is about seventy-five years old. She managed to convince the elders in council to retire her. I still don't know how she did it. It's eminent that soon her hubby of ninety-five years old would likely join his ancestors in any moment, and she desires to mourn him and perform the rites as his first wife and only wife. He devoted his life to her. And he did not have any other woman bear children for him. She did not cook, wash or clean after him, but he did not mind. In fact, he did these things for her in order for her to be free to perform her duties. They say she was the best care-giver in the past years, and I say the love of a man brought out the good in her.

Sitting at my Grandma's compound listening to her endless tales of the strange stories that surround our village, we heard an uproar. Following our survival instincts we first of all ran into the house and ducked. Then came out head first, checking the terrain to see if we were safe to do so. When we perceived the coast was clear, we summoned courage and stepped out quietly not making any sound with our bare feet. We got to the gate and we were told that some strangers had been caught picking snails. At the mention of it, my Grandma screamed and held her head with both hands obviously indicating that disaster looms. When I asked why, she explained that it is forbidden to pick snails or eat snails from our village. Grandma went on to explain that snails are allowed to move about freely without being killed. I was like seriously? Is that why we never get to eat them? I told my Grandma that I heard they are very delicious and she covered my mouth very fast to prevent others from hearing me mention those abominable words. She went on to explain the reason being that during the war, when they(the villagers) run away to secure hideouts that the snails all come out and wipe off their footsteps, hence making it impossible for the enemy to locate their where about.

My Grandma refused to let us go to the village square but my siblings and I sneaked out to watch how the elders will decide their fate. As we had been told, the penalty is death. But it's not spoken out directly when the verdict is given but they do it in a coded language that even the defaulters have no knowledge of what lay ahead of them. As we watched keenly, the strangers were asked to be taken away and it looked like they will be taken to prison, but death is usually the end game

As we stood there I pondered. To be killed over a mere snail? That's ludicrous!!! I thought to myself, stealing a line from one of my favorite movie. As the crowd was dispersed, we turned to leave but a very strong hand held me back.

"She came! She came!!! I told you that she would come!!!"

The man holding my hand kept shouting out loud. I struggled to be set free but to no avail. I instructed my siblings to run and get me my grandma. This was a misunderstanding. We were only visiting the village for the first time since we were born. It was ironic the way my father just woke us up one blessed day and requested that I should arrange our luggage because we were going to the village. This is how we got here.

I was taken to a hut, and asked to seat outside on a stool. It was a long wait. My grandma arrived and she was briefed on my being the "Chosen One".

"Chosen for what?" I interrupted them.

I was shunned by different angry voices who were probably shocked at my guts. City life has taught me to speak my mind, where as in the village I am to wait to be spoken to. I dare not speak when elders are speaking. And being a woman, I should be seen not heard.

Everything went so fast. Soon my parents were summoned by the elders, my Granny was included. When they returned, my mum's eyes were all swollen. I was told I would be the new caregiver of the sacred snake. That translated to so many things. But major issues came to my mind.

The First been that; I would have to remain 'forever' in the village.

Two, I won't have the experience and enjoy the pleasures of motherhood.

Three, Education is to be thrown out the window.

Four, Am the only child (Biological) of my parents, the rest of my siblings were adopted when my parents couldn't conceive after me. So who would bury my parents? Who would mourn them? Since I am not allowed to shed a tear and not permitted to cry.

Also I would marry a man, who would definitely marry another woman after me. That is, I will have to indulge in polygamy. This is too much for me. My heart felt like it would swell up and burst into a thousand shreds. Where would I see a man of my taste in the village? The type of man my heart longs for wouldn't even consider polygamy. So emotionally I am done for. From all indication I would have to settle for what the village offers. This unexposed lot! There's no bank or recreational activities in my village. All they do is local stuffs. Their mediocrity won't even let them invite development in to their circle. But luckily we have telecommunication but with a poor network.

There are so many heart breaking issues. I didn't know how to begin to cry out! I had longed for years to be a pediatrician. I just love children, now what?

I refused the so called job vehemently and I told my parents they should leave the elders to source for a village girl who would be glad to dedicate her life to a cause she believes in. But for me it's a no-no.

It's so absurd. I never knew such mediocrity still existed! And worst still, that it could be shoved down my throat and I wouldn't have the right to reject it.

When last was a war fought? I asked myself, when? When last did such happen? What's the essence of keeping a snake when they are so many resources at our beck and call that can be utilized at will? What happened to satellites and the likes?

I refused to be part of such arrant nonsense. I was warned that very deadly consequences awaits anyone that rejects the offer. One example from the past, was a lady who buried thirty seven of her family members. All extended family, cousins, nieces, in-laws all wiped out. At the annoying end of that story, she still ended up being the Caregiver to the sacred snake. What kind of issue is this? I lamented within me.

Another I was told, traveled out of Nigeria and ran to neighboring countries. But she was brought home in a dilapidated state. She could not move, eat and talk. She was covered all over by boils and she smelt like she was a corpse already decaying. They say immediately the vehicle that brought her entered the boundary of the village, she started recuperating fast and by the time the vehicle drove into her father's compound, she was hale and hearty. Her skin as smooth as a baby's.

I told them that all these are plots to scare me and I refused to be scared. I maintained my stand.

According to tradition, I guess to avoid the total annihilation of my entire family as witnessed before, my parents and family were advised to go for ritual cleansing to separate themselves from the effects of my rejecting the service to the sacred snake.

It's been one year and I have faced and passed through countless challenges.

My boyfriend who I loved with all my life, broke up with me without reason. My schools scholarship board rejected my application to study for my master's degree despite my position as the best graduating student in my class. To top that my whole university result from part one to graduation mysteriously disappeared from my schools exams and record department. There was no record of me. It now seem like I was never there. Wherever I go, people are put off by my presence. It felt like there's an aura around me that causes chaos. There are always negative and irritating issues surrounding me.

In this one year alone, I have been accused of stealing forty eight times, almost on a weekly basis. I have come to know all the police officers working in my surrounding because almost all of them have at one time or the other been in charge of my case. I can't put to words the height of my embarrassment. I have lost all credibility.

I also have a white growth on my tongue that's spreading everywhere around my mouth. The pain is unbearable and the smell so awful. I can't chew, neither can any food that has taste pass through my throat. I am forced to take liquids and the food I get to eat are bland. If I have to eat meat, it has to be cooked till very soft and with no spice at all. Even my potatoes have to be mashed. Life was unbearable.

My parents have begged me without relenting to accept the offer. That my life is the priority. And tried to convince me that things are changing that the lady who was there now will be allowed to retire and she will have the luxury of spending her last days with her husband.

They said even the gods are becoming exposed. That as times are changing even the gods are adapting to the changes. That prior to this time, a married woman on a motor bike (means of transportation) with legs spread behind a man not her husband and her boobs nudging on his back as he rides would have been dealt a death sentence half a century ago. But today, the gods know better too.

I finally agreed to go to the village to see what awaits me. I was brought in to the village today. As soon as I crossed the boundary and entered the land, the entire sore in my mouth disappeared. I was whole again. I could see and think clearly. The clutter in my head was gone. I sat upright and looked at my surroundings. I had no idea who was in the car with me, but after then I could comprehend everything well. I noticed the village ad slight changes as the car drove further down the road, I felt my phone vibrate and I opened to take a look. I noticed the network in the village was stronger than even I had anticipated. I checked to see that my iPad was browsing- a smile danced around my lips. My mum noticed and gave me a very tight hug.

As we drove by I saw one huge building. I stretched to see that it was a business plaza that housed two banks, from what I could see from the sign post. And there was a fast-food outlet too.

We finally got to our destination which was the shrine of the scared snake. The Elders were all seated and waiting. And I noticed that a bunch of onlookers where there also. For the first time in a year I wasn't the least concerned about the thoughts of people or what tomorrow held. I was just too happy to be pain free. All I wanted was a very delicious meal. As If they were mind readers they asked if I needed anything. I told them I needed to eat. I told them what I would love to eat and someone returned almost immediately with the food. God! I cleaned my mouth and sat down to devour the food. They all sat and waited so patiently for me to finish. I felt like a queen.

When I was set to face my duties, they welcomed me properly and did all the traditional rites to cleanse me. My attire was changed to something befitting my new status. They sat me down and told me the history of the snake again and its relevance to the community.

Then finally, I got to see the snake. I was shocked to see how old it was. I was told it can't move about anymore. And to my hearts delight, they were sad that it won't live another twenty years. The oracle has said that I would be the last caregiver. I could have asked them to introduce veterinary medicine, to help take better care of the snake but won't that be me prolonging my sorrow?

I just turned twenty one and wise in my own eyes. Everything was made available for my comfort. I was given a piece of land and my parents brought in an architect (a local builder in my opinion) to draw out a structure to suit my needs. I desired a very well furnished two bed bungalow. It has to have a study, a gymnasium and a walk in closet plus a gigantic bathroom with the best Jacuzzi bath ever. I had a blank cheque so all I desired I would surely have.

I had an unbelievable monthly allowance of two hundred and twenty five thousand naira. Talk about over-compensation. Asides that, I don't buy food. Any thing I want is been brought to me free. I have servants who cater to my every need. If I choose not to marry, I have the authority to mandate any man of my choice to come sleep with me. This is serious. I am also free to dispose of him as I choose. The sex life of the caregiver is an abomination to talk about.

I have few hours everyday where I can go out of the compound. Then once every quarter I am to be given a twenty four hours break to travel out of the village to anywhere of my choice (This was added newly).

With all the information I now have, I began setting my goals for the first ten years. Amongst them is to get my master's degree online for the first two years. My university results that mysteriously disappeared has been seen and mailed to me. Then the other eight years, I would study other professional courses. I am going to build a library. I have no access to religious activities of my choice. But I have access and can watch from my iPad and read whatever I choose. The snake as I have come to notice sleeps very long hours and eats very little. I will make an extra one hundred thousand naira per quarter on its feeding. Since it does not leave its tree anymore, there is less to be done. Which translates into more study time for me.

I was told a huge mall housing several multinational supermarkets/ shops has been opened in a major city close by. Forty five minutes away to be precise. I know where my quarterly twenty hours break would be spent. I can see myself in Spa being pampered. Also I will have the means to go shopping to my heart's content. I also have a travel allowance of hundred thousand naira per quarter. Where do they generate all this cash from? This thought have crossed my mind countless times.

With technology at my fingertips, I can get whatever I desire. All I have to do is search online for whatever I need and it will be shipped to my location. Did I mention that I am to get a lot of freebies? This is how. Whenever the village is given substantial amount of money from cooperate bodies and multinationals/oil companies (it's in an oil producing area) a sizeable amount is given to the snake and I as the caregiver has sole custody of the money. I own it because I am the snake's next of kin. So it's mine to keep. I was told the last caregiver was given ten million naira block. I imagine now that she has retired from active duty she would spend her last days in luxury.

I am treated like a queen. When I go into the village people bow as I walk by. Some sing praises of me. The woman who gives up all her rights to serve the interest of the people. Its going to take a while getting used to it.

My parents promised to visit twice a month. My Grandma has moved in with me. I didn't know that was permitted. She gave the excuse of been my translator for I can't speak the local dialect. She has also started teaching me to speak in our local tongue. I get to chat with friends online. The change wasn't as tragic as I thought. I tell everyone I got a local appointment.

I see potentials. I am going to help my village talk to the government. There are a lot of issues that needs to be attended to. But I will have to begin from the renovation of schools. And I also intend to assist bring one or two infrastructure to the village. I am going to use these challenge to my advantage. I won't let my life be ruined with misery just because I was chosen by the gods for this difficult tasks. I am going to turn this into my own success story. Who knows I may

run for office in the future. in twenty years the snake will be history
and I will be turning forty one. That's not too late to build on the life
I would have already developed for myself. So many angles to explore
but one day at a time.

Africa my Africa!! I hail!!

NDUDI

STORY 13

Amina's Story

I sat down on the floor of the cold and dark room. My body has adjusted to the temperature of the room and it was no longer an issue for me. The room has only one window and it was shut. I cannot remember if it was a block house or a mud hut. I was not myself when I was brought here. As I sat down counting the seconds to when this whole nightmare will end, I heard footsteps approaching and then it stopped. I knew instantly who it was that was standing outside. That should be none other than my mate that I am very close to. She must have stopped to survey the terrain before she comes closer to the door. If she is caught trying to make contact with me she will be dealt with mercilessly.

I didn't have to wait for long before I heard something slide under the door. I crawled towards it and was filled with joy to see that it's my phone. How could she have known? God bless her soul. I switched on the phone and began going through it. I saw a buzz on the internet #being female in Naija#. I decided to see what it's all about. A particular quote caught my attention. It's a tweet and the tweet said #being female naija… "My grandma had to spend three days with my Grandpa's corpse." I smiled.

The way she said it, one would think that it's a thing of the past and I believe she too must feel it happened once upon a time. Like maybe half a century ago. Anyone would have felt the same because of the new levels of exposure we claim to adopt. Trends are changing. Manner of approaching issues are also changing. So I wouldn't blame her or anyone if they thought that it happened in the past.

First I want to appreciate the Warmate book club Abuja Nigeria for discussing such a topic. Like I read, it started while they were reviewing "Chimamanda Adichie's" book and they were lead to share the message on their Whatsapp from there – it went viral. Am so glad such issues are brought up because Nigerian women pass through a lot. Cultures are a bit unfair to us. Am not castigating my culture or condemning it because I feel at the time it was made, it was the level of exposure and happenings of the people then that led them to make such laws. But now we are claiming to be exposed they should please cut us some slacks.

I married Dumebi from eastern Nigeria. While I am from the northern part of our country. His parents where born in the north, and also was He. His grand parents and some of his extended family all reside in different parts of the state. They have quite a number of branches of the business they are running spread around the northern states. This meant that quite a large number of his relatives and easterners reside in the north with us. So I didn't have the need to travel down to the eastern part because virtually every member of his family resided in the north with us. Hence my dowry was paid without me visiting his village for familiarization. My wedding was a two week colorful ceremony. A lot of his people came from the village. And the Igbo Community was fully represented. My family compound was filled to capacity. It was a carnival of sorts.

Dumebi was a second generation of Ibos, born in the north. He has not spent time in his village except for the yearly returns. But after marriage, Dumebi has stayed back on two occasions and went without me for one. We were married three years and eight months.

Yes were! Dumebi died five days ago.

In these five days, my life has turned around. It was to me like; God turned his back to me.

Dumebi and I had no issues yet. He was younger than me with two years but one would not know. No one said my age was an issue. We all grew up together and we all knew who was born when.

Dumebi brought a world of experience into his family business. He did not have a university degree because he stopped schooling at Junior Secondary School II. So he didn't have a senior school leaving certificate. All he had was a primary school certificate. But he committed himself fully to the family business and brought in radical changes.

I on the other hand read Business Administration and have a Masters degree in Strategic marketing. I was a privileged child. I studied at the best schools. I was raised well. Dumebi was my first Love and I couldn't envision the future without him. With him it was just love. I had better education, better exposure, rich parents and a good job at a superb bank. My salary was over two thousand dollars per month, because I got promoted repeatedly and I have a very good and progressive profile. Having read Strategic Marketing from a good University in Scotland, I had it easy with raking in clients for my bank. I was a member of different professional bodies.

On my own I was solid. All I needed was the love of a supportive husband. And I got it. Dumebi was the answer to my prayers. God was merciful to me.

Our love was near perfect. We were two different people from two different worlds but complemented each other beautifully. I was secured financially and emotionally. He was making money too. And Dumebi was much focused. My Certificates did not in any way intimidate him. My financial stability was not an issue. We lived transparently and had nothing to hide. Life was peaceful... my Dreams were valid.

Then the day of his birthday this year, I threw him a surprise party. It was well attended. Dumebi danced like never before. He was so happy and everyone commented on how cheerful and lively a celebrant he was. My friends secretly whispered in my ears that I was the luckiest woman alive. And I never doubted for a second. We went to bed. Only I woke up. We didn't even make love. He said he was too tired. And I let him sleep.

Pardon me for making the story short, I just feel too weak for long and in-depth explanations. Since that morning till now, everything has been hazy. Dumebi has always hated mortuaries and kept repeating that he would never be in one.

Thus his wishes were granted. After he was confirmed dead, a comprehensive embalmment was done on him that could last for a month. I tried to make them do an autopsy to know the cause of death. He has never been sick and he was healthy the night before. But the parents wouldn't hear of it. After embalmment, the next day we all proceeded to the village.

On getting there, I got silent treatments and cold shoulders from his distant relatives. There was a theory on ground that I killed Dumebi. At first his family wouldn't hear of it but soon his family that lived with me in the north and knew me all my life bought into the conspiracy. I was alienated. I came alone with no one from my family. I didn't feel the need because his sisters and cousins were my best friends. We had decided that the date of the burial will be communicated to my family.

The burial date was fixed but first there where rites I had to perform. I was to sleep with Dumebi's Corpse for three days. And it is believed that if I killed him I would be tormented to confess. It was a psychological theory that could yield results if it where true.

But what could I gain from killing Dumebi. He was my Crown. He was the icing on my cake. He completed everything in me. One of my mates (Mates in Nigerian usually refers to women married to brothers or cousins.) managed to sneak in to me, my phone and iPad fully charged so I can keep my mind of off things. The first day, I cried nonstop. I cried for Dumebi's short life. I cried for his dreams that were aborted. I cried that we never get to spend enough quality time together. I cried that I have lost the love of my life. I cried because I was not sure I could ever get a man as good as he again. What's the chance that I will be two times lucky? I ached that I had no kids with him to remember him by. He was my best friend, my confidant, my greatest fan. He motivated me daily and pushed me to greater heights. Now how do I cope? I cried and cried and cried.

By the second day, I kind of got closure. I was calmer. Reality had sinked in. My heart was ready for the healing process. I saw him in my dreams asking me to be strong for me and our babies. I was shocked. And he told me yes, that we are pregnant. That he left everything to me in his will and he made sure his parents are catered for too. That there's nothing to be worried about.

The morning of the third day, I began vomiting and suspicious eyes where all over me. I asked them to get me a pregnancy test strip. Almost an hour later, I was given the strip. With the early morning urine I saved, I tested with it and true to my dream; a very bold positive line came on. And shouts of joy filled the air. I was immediately bundled into a bathing facility, from where hot water presented itself from where; I don't know.

I was bathed and fed properly. I turned from a murder suspect to a very prized possession in matter of minutes.

My mother-in-law sent for a vehicle that took me to their health Centre where I was confirmed eight weeks pregnant. And they where two heart beats!! Twins!!! My mother-in -law went on to roll on the floor with joy. Dumebi had left her with something to hold on to. Not one but two. And she openly prayed that they turn out to be boys; typical Nigerian woman.

The burial has come and gone. Everything went smoothly. I did not tell anyone in my family what I was made to go through. I bore it in secret and it will go with me to my grave. Even my kids won't hear of it. Maybe many other widows out there share same sentiments that could be the reason why it's not out in the open. But it still goes on.

I didn't want to judge the culture and traditions of my in-laws but in their pain and in search of justice they can mar innocent women for life. I have made plans to fly to the U.K. There I will have series of therapy sessions to put my mind at ease.

So now my own contribution to #Beingfemaleinnaija. "Being female in naija is very tasking but what does not kill you makes you strong. We have mastered the act of overcoming all that is thrown our way"

STORY 14

Chiamaka's Story

It's our eighteenth wedding anniversary. And there's nothing to celebrate. Asides the fact of been alive and my hubby and I been gainfully employed; translating to our being financially stable. But what is money without any children of our own to lavish it on?

Marriage has recently become a nightmare. Nonso my husband has lost every interest in me, and I don't hold anything against him. Tests have proven we are both very okay. No issues whatever and we should have loads of children.

We have done all, but medicine has failed us and I don't believe in divorce but the thought of staying alive having no children is unbearable. I love kids and my hubby loves them even more.

I have not conceived once in these eighteen years of marriage. We married at twenty-two and twenty-seven respectively. Nonso, being five years older than me. He met me a virgin and he married me so. That has been a saving grace on its own because everyone is aware that countless abortions are not the reason for my childlessness.

Not a day goes by without me been depressed and crying. Crying that I did not hasten to the word of the elders. If only I had listened, today I would have been a mother to children. I would have enjoyed three to four full term pregnancies and enjoyed raising three to four kids.

I can't think of adoption. I just can't. I long to experience carrying my own children. With my own genes running in them. I desire to feel fulfilled. I feel somehow lesser than a woman. My self-esteem is been pulverized. I see young nieces, cousins, neighbors get married and puff! Big protruding belles and childbirth all around. I have lost counts. In eighteen years, every single one around us has had kids. Soon these kids would start having their own kids. I can't keep a smiling face. I have changed. The pain and longings are having a great toll on my psych. My skin, my hair and my nails are all suffering. Laughter is truly the best medicine and sorrow eats up the bones. When I look in the mirror, it's like I have faded. Suddenly, there's no joy, no happy smiles, I just look lost and empty. How can Nonso live with someone like this?

Sex has become work. It's like a doctor's appointment that needs to be fulfilled. The days am ovulating and either of us miss out, it's like the heavens should fall, because we are tormented by the fact that pregnancy could have taken place that day. We keep appointments on sex. I have a calendar for monitoring my ovulation period. And we follow all sex rules faithfully yet year after year not one month was my period delayed even for a day. The day am to see it, as early as five am in the morning, my period awakes me. And that whole day, whole week and the proceeding days that lead to the next ovulation day are all gloomy. It like a switch goes off.

I had secretly gone with my mother to places (Spiritual places) to find out if there's another underlying factor. And I got same answers in about twenty places I visited over the years. They all said exact same thing. That we are under a curse, a voodoo curse.

Many years back, there was a feud between two families. It was so terrible, that it led to a female member of one of the family been buried alive. As she was thrown in the grave and sand was thrown over her, she continued to declare her innocence and began to swear. She swore that anyone from her clan, especially from her lineage that marries from the other family shall remain fruitless for the rest of their lives. She swore it repeatedly, and cried bitterly asking Mother Nature to defend her.

And true to her curses, after then anyone, woman or man who claims to be in love with each other from any of these families, have faced tremendous hardship. There has been too much emotional baggage and stress. It was said that Ninety-three percent of the marriage pack up. And both parties end up going into another marriage where they bear children at speedy rates.

I was told that, if I slept with another man, I would become pregnant instantly. So goes for my hubby. But the two of us will never yield any fruit. Now that I am turning forty, with little child-bearing age left, am beginning to have double mind. My hubby has stood by me through it all. He is turning forty five too and no children. By now we are suppose to have kids that are getting ready to graduate from the university. He also desires them too. I know West Africa permits men not only to cheat on their wives but to marry as much as they desire.

Friends and family have all been chipping in their two kobo. They are all of the opinion that Nonso has children elsewhere. Our part of the Country does not have ancestors who frown on adultery, so nothing should hold me back; they advised. And lucky me, because women from other parts dare not sleep outside their matrimonial home, or they will be dealt horrendous consequences. She may loose her husband or her life or the child she bears. But nothing holds me back... That's in their opinion, anyways. But I am the kind of woman who likes to finish anything she starts. If it's going to end, it should not be from me. Nonso should end it. And in all honesty, I love my husband and do not want to start something that can be broken so easily.

I have spent years working hard. I work in a multi-national, doing very good for my self. I have built four houses, own some other choice properties that include a very thriving car wash business with branches all over town. On the car wash business alone I rake in an average of forty five thousand a day. When sales are up, I make up to one hundred and fifty thousand naira (about one thousand dollars) a day. I also own a catering outfit with twenty food vendor personnel's.

I have cooks, who prepare meals every day, Monday – Sundays. After cooking; they share among twenty food carts. These young men push their carts to different locations. Some stay at busy markets, others at schools and the rest at busy motor parks. And usually before twelve in the afternoon, Seventy percent of them are through with sales. I make steady two hundred thousand naira daily, but I have to run expenses from there. At the end of the month though I make about six million naira and have a running expense of three and a half million naira.

I also have a distributorship in the leading soft drink in Nigeria. I make a minimum of three hundred thousand naira on rebate monthly. Peak periods could yield almost a million or a little above per month. I have a Bridal Shop where I sell and hire out foreign styled wedding gowns. I sell bridal accessories and do event decorations and bake wedding cakes. I have my hands full and all businesses are raking in very good money. I have a bank balance that is always in excess of sixty million naira. Asides that account, every other business I registered under my hubby's company. He owns sixty percent, I own forty. The houses, the land, the cars all built and bought with Nonso's name. Point to note he also chipped in a bit once in a while.

I did it to make him secure and give me peace. Nigerian men are the worst bred. (A good percentage of them though) They are Chauvinistic and the ones that do work, expect their wives to be seen but not heard. I have friends who totally depend on their husbands. When cooking gas runs out and they call their husbands, the wicked and arrogant men will respond..." The gas is finished and so? Did you bring gas from your father's house? Or did you use gas in your father's house? Your mum till date, does she own a gas cooker? Or when they ask to use the family vehicle because of the number of children he decided they must have, I mean see Oghale! To move about with five children is not easy yet the hubby will respond to her request to borrow the family vehicle car is usually like this; Car? Did your mother drive a car with the eight of you she gave birth to? Has your father ever owned a tire?

Many women are verbally and emotionally abused because they let themselves be slaves and are too lazy to work. Fine, men are not supposed to treat women so unjustly, but I still hold my stand that when you know the tendency of men in your country, you have to sit up and act smart. 'No dulling' as we say here in Nigeria.

I have a joint account with my hubby, but the account with the sixty million and counting, he has no idea of. I also have my salaried account I have not touched for fifteen years. I only borrow from there and put back. He knows about that. That account is a few tens of thousands away from thirty million naira. He knows about that but I have kept my foot down about that. No going there! No way!

The houses in his name were mistakes on my part. I had built those houses, thinking my kids would grow up to inherit everything. But now I know better. Am not a bad woman because when people (naija people) hear this, they will be like …. She's stingy and wicked. But when men do same to women, it's not a problem.

I have an aunty who struggled with the husband for thirty years. She has four kids and at age sixty-three, when she has retired and decided it's time to rest and travel the world in the arms of her husband, the hubby took a young lady as wife. A girl thirty-five years, her hubby's junior. And this young lady pumped out four kids in five years; all boys. Everything my Aunty worked for was gone. Everything she did with the husband was in his name, she did not keep any money to herself. All her salaries went in to start different business and the proceeds used to train their kids. Now the last of them just got married only for the hubby to begin life all over again buying pampers, sending children to kindergarten. Going to hospitals to and fro doing immunizations and tendering to teething problems. All using the cash, he and my aunty worked for. My Aunty, broken hearted relocated to Germany to reside with her eldest daughter.

Another distant relative of mine, only found out about her hubby's other family, at the family compound where meeting was held to discuss burial arrangements of her late husband. She saw kids looking all like her kids running about. Shocked, she asked whose children they were. And she got the shock of her life.

Now the late hubby was a stay at home dad. He worked from home. He never owned an office space nor did any nine-to-five job all through his life. And the amazing thing is her hubby never slept out. And they was never a day, she returned home from her office, without meeting him at home. He was the perfect husband.

The annoying fact was that, it was not as if, she had all her kids then this woman had hers. No! They had them all together. The first daughter of my Aunty was born on her own. Born alone with no one sharing the same time frame as her. The second child of my distant aunty and the ladies first child were same year, only months apart. The third child of my aunty and the second child of this lady are a year apart. My auntie's last child and the lady's twins, where also same year.

At the family meeting, it was announced that the first son was to inherit the mansion the father lived in. My aunty had the first son who was just a few months older than the other lady's first son. Mphew!! My aunty escaped been asked to moved out of the house she suffered to build by whiskers. Where would she and her kids have gone to? She sat in silence, listened and watched as her properties where dissected among these kids. My aunty having only one son did not have much. The other lady having three sons got quite a chunk of the properties.

She listened as choice properties in luxury areas where given out those kids while her daughters were made to share one building with three apartment – that is, three to one. The small twins had a full office complex each and the other son, the old mansion they lived in before they moved to the present one they now live in; the one they were lucky to have retained.

In minutes, my distant Aunt lost all she worked for with her husband. I don't think they both worked for it, the hubby was always home. While she went out in search of daily bread. Anyway, that can be seen as a contribution on his part.

She kept wishing she could kill the wicked dead man all over again.

What time did he go out to visit and run another family? To think that this went on for decades without her knowing, hurt her beyond words.

Another tale, I am conversant with, is that of a dear friend who works while the hubby was jobless for over ten years. He had a son before he met her, but he has refused for years to acknowledge the boy. My friend did not relent in fighting for what she believed to be right. She buys clothes and sends to this child. But over the years, the man has remained nonchalant towards this boy. Point to note, my friend has four girls. No male issues. She solely fought and raised money to register a company for him and made sure he sits up. Soon with the help of her friends she got him a good long term contract. Cash started coming in and he demanded she quit her job and be home full time. She obeyed. Soon they had enough to get a beautiful home in a sophiscated part of town. While moving their stuff, she came in contact with the company documents. Which she suddenly realize, that she has never seen. And she never bothered to ask. She provided the money and the contact to make the application but she did not follow through. He gave her the part to sign. She did and never saw the percentage given her, not until that fateful Saturday morning.

The registration of the company had one million shares. Her hubby owned forty (40%) percent, and a name she recognized to be the son's name also owned forty (40%) percent. While she and her four daughters where squeezed into twenty percent. My friend turned white. She wondered if this is not the same son he has refused to acknowledge.

In Nigeria, the sons inherit all personal possessions of the father. If this boy was to take forty percent for himself, then on event of the death of her spouse, he is also by right going to claim the forty percent owned by the father. Now adding that to his forty means he would claim eighty percent of the business; plus the fathers' personal house, cars and other properties. She wondered; if he could share his company like this, then his will and final testaments will also be same. The lady in particular kept mute about what she saw and she went to work on how to secure the future of her kids. She started doing business and made plans to build a house and make sure to save money in the accounts she intended to open for each daughter. She also made plans to have the kids learn two or more handiwork. It could be hairdressing, tailoring, baking etc. but her daughters won't grow to be a liability to themselves and any man.

After my awareness of all these stories, I was determined not to allow nature repeat its course. Yes, I made mistakes on assuming I would have children. But I had plans. I tried to talk to my husband about others ways we could exploit but he wouldn't bulge. My hubby has disagreed to using a surrogate. In Nigeria, the hubby makes the decision most times and it's final.

Most times I am tempted to feel, he doesn't care. Or maybe he is nonchalant because he has his own plans. But I leave everything to God!

Months later.....

So many things have happened in the past nine months... I listened to a cd by Mike Murdock and I agreed with him that leaving everything to God is a lazy man's way. God's time is usually the time we stand up, dust ourselves off and move!! I called Nonso one evening and told him am flying abroad to have my eggs saved before time passes me by. And I suggested to him to follow me so that, together we can get a surrogate. He blatantly refused. I said fine and went ahead to travel with his knowledge though. I got sperm donors from a sperm bank and got three surrogates. The whole process was expensive but who cares? I have got money! Idle money that's just lying around, waiting to be spent. After about two months, I got three babies on the way. One from a Swedish American. Another from Costa-Rica and the last from Bangladesh. No one will accuse me of adultery. They are all my babies. I returned to Nigeria in the third month.

Few weeks after I got back from my trip. I got a rude shock. It got to my hearing that Nonso is under serious stress by the family of a lady that bore children for him. According to the information I got, the lady died about two weeks from the day I got the information. She died immediately after childbirth, the baby is alive though. But that is not the issue on ground. Nonso's cousin who narrated the tale said, this is the third child the said lady has for him. And they are all boys. The first son is about nine years old at the time I was told. The second son is going to be five. Then now, this last one. Why the spacing? I wondered. The issue on ground now is that the family of the late lady has demanded that Nonso marry the deceased.

A marriage ceremony will be conducted and her bride price will be paid. Entertainment will go on as usual and every traditional rite sealed. Nonso had refused and he was told that if he doesn't pay, there's no way, he can have access to his sons. The names of the children will cease to be his as they will bear the names of their maternal grandfather. I was overwhelmed.

I kept quite pretending not to know the latest development. But I had told Nonso of my three peas in the pod. In a few months I would welcome three children. When I told him, he kept mute and never uttered any word. Many would say my financial status intimidated him but in truth that was not the case. Nonso was naturally a very calm and quiet person, one who doesn't want stress of any sort. I am even surprised that he could do this to me. This is because he has no bone in his body to plan evil against anyone or hurt anyone. I guessed he had enough solid backing from his family for him to be able to push through with this.

We remained together, existing as man and wife. No quarrels or scruples. I was my vibrant self again and full of life because now I have something to look forward to. I was told he went to pay the dowry of the dead woman and his family went with him to the girl's village that is five hours away. It involved crossing a river, so they could not return that day. I had all night to think of what to do. For the Last ten years, I have been a fool. Living with a man who was breeding sons outside while I remain at home, with him knowing fully well the consequences of every thing.

The morning after, I called my mother who's just turning sixty and I briefed her on the food vendor business. I asked my manager to report to my mum hence-forth. I opened an account for that and monitored the business. I also drafted a partnership agreement for the distributorship where I will get fifty percent of sales per month. I also created an account that the cash will be deposited into. Then I sold three quarter of the lands I bought and got about one hundred million from them. The cash I used to buy three choice properties,

I intended to build event centers on. The event centre didn't take much in comparison to erecting an apartment building. I easily and quickly completed one. And took the other two to decking levels and left them there. I would raise them up and complete them as cash flows in monthly.

I made down payments for three two-bed apartment abroad. Making an advance payment of seventy-five percent of the price upfront. The balance twenty-five percent I would complete in twenty four months.

I sold my eighteen million naira jeep and added cash to it, bought an apartment in another choice country, where I get rents about two hundred thousand naira monthly. I told Nonso I would be relocating and he is welcomed to visit anytime he chose. And yet again, in his calm nature said nothing. Every other thing I left the same. After all he has three sons to take care of. He knew I was very fair.

Years later...

Nonso relocated abroad. He never fought with me. But kept quiet all through the years. This is a part of Nonso I would never trade for anything. A lot of people may see him as a weakling but that weakness is also his greatest strength. We had no one except each other for more than two decades and we couldn't live without one another. Our lives were synced. After I left, he came over and we discussed. We were able to come to a peaceful compromise. And life went on. We were together through the births of my kids. We decided to have all three kids born on same day. He adopted my three kids. And we named them after him. My three kids are celebrating their fourth birthday soon. I had two girls and a boy. All mixed breed.

I requested he bring his children over. He did. We now live together in one big mansion. All our children's future well insured. I have paid all my outstanding mortgages and cash comes in from left, right and centre. Foreign land favored Nonso a lot. It was like his destiny was hindered in Nigeria. Choice company's battled to have him. The two top companies negotiated with each other, one was to have him on full time basis and the other on consultation basis. I need not tell you that he rakes in loads of hard currency monthly.

I didn't have any problems during these period, although I had some emotional and psychological issues. But Nonso's quiet disposition helped lot. And I had this unshakable faith in him that he is a good person, so it was easy for me to see his decision as not one aimed to hurt me because I knew him deep that he couldn't hurt anyone intentional. It made forgiving very easy. And trust was easily rebuilt. People say it's also because I am financially stable. And I agree too. I had enough cash to walk the talk. The case would have been dangerously difficult had I been penniless. And my heart goes out to many of my Nigerians wives who have no penny to their names and thus can't see a way out of their problems.

Women that are less privileged would have gone through hell and continue going through hell. That's the plight of thousands of women, living in Nigeria.

They know no other life. So they adapt. Well, all I can say is thank you Lord, for my story is different.

Chiamaka

AFTER THOUGHT

The aim of this book is not to criticize, ridicule or start a platform that seeks to change our Nigerian culture. All I am soliciting for is for women to empower themselves; by bettering their lives wherever they find themselves. They should not allow whatever misery they are passing through to swallow them up.

When you live in a country where you are govern by customs and traditions aging far back four generations-plus, my candid advice and plea is to practice **"strategic thinking"**. We should apply it to every facet of our lives and with perseverance we would soon see positive changes.

Tantamount to this, is the dire need for us to teach our daughters how to be independent from their prime. We should inculcate the desire to make something out of life for themselves. Women should stop "dulling" and wake up and start thinking.

I recommend the book titled "Thinking for a change" – by John C. Maxwell. You can't change the laws in your land within an instant. If the customs have to change, it will happen in the process of time, and may take tens of decades to evolve.

Now that you are caught up in whatever cross fire, my stand is, don't be drowned with it. Cry! Cry if you must. If you need to let go of some pent up emotions, please do CRY. It is therapeutic. But after having a good cry, dust yourself off. Sit down, lie down or go for a walk; a stroll. In the process – Think! Think!! Think!!! But dearly beloved, please think "STRATEGICALLY" think "CONSTRUCTIVELY" think "REALISTICALLY" think "POSSIBILITY" think "CREATIVELY" think "REFLECTIVELY" think! Think!! Think!!! And BE FOCUSED!!

I have noticed something amusing for a while now. About five widows I know personally that lost their hubbies within the space of six months to one year have evolved beautifully. You see a beautiful glow in them. Their eyes light up. Their smiles...contagious. When you spend few minutes with these widows, you see a brand new woman. They dress better, their skin looks healthier. They now socialize whole-heartedly. They walk with their heads high. Take a minute and try to visualize one or two widows aged twenty-five to fifty that you know. Look closely and you will be shocked at the transformation. You may even pass by one you know quite well everyday, but you unintentionally refused to accept the image you see now with the one you were familiar with. That forty-two year old mother of four that used to look sixty has now evolved into a beautiful damsel, looking thirty.

I don't know how to draw a conclusion on this matter... is it that the marriages were bad for their emotional and physical health? Was it marriage in itself that was bad or the character, ego and habits of the departed husband that made them look haggard and feel lost. Is it the determination by these women to deal with the challenges of their marriage no matter what, that sucks the life out of them?

Not only do the widows look good, even their kids begin looking fabulously refreshed. They now participate in extra curricular activities and no longer act and look timid. I have experienced a few cases. And it's mind boggling.

Do these men have to lose their lives for these women to get a grip of life once more? There has to be another way out and I don't mean Divorce, because to me that is another world of its own. I personally do not see anything wrong with letting go of a bond that threatens to terminate the peace and quiet of a woman's life but hey! That's my own opinion. And I have no intention of forcing a decision down your throat. Even the holy book says God gives us choices. And went further to say we should choose life. In Nigeria we say; you hold the knife, you hold the yam (vegetable) so cut it up as you desire.

Back to what I was saying earlier; It's my belief that strategic thinking combined with been down to earth realistic about your situation you can map out a plan to better your life. But it all boils down to decision.

Ben Stein said it clearly "The indispensable first step to getting the things you want out of life is this! Decide what you want!!

Do you desire a better life? Do you long to pursue those dreams? Or you would settle for mediocrity, blaming everyone from nature to family to the kind of hubby you married for the wrong turn of things in your life.

"Mediocrity is always a personal choice" – John. C. Maxwell. Evaluate your situation. Do not lie to yourself. Tell it as it is – "Too many people rush to solutions, and as a result, they end up solving the wrong problem" – J.C. Maxwell.

Look at your challenge thoroughly. Take your resources into consideration. If there is no income, work on a plan to generate income for your self – been independent is the way to go. After you put things on ground that provides you with cash flow, realistically strategize yourself out of that hole.

"A strategy that doesn't take into account resources is doomed to failure – John C. Maxwell.

One of the objectives of these stories is to tell the tale from the horse's mouth and thus showcase how things are on the other side of fence. You thought it was greener right? One woman always feels the other is luckier. A huge percentage though.

Now, my goal here is to force women to look for possibilities in every kind of situation they find themselves. Every woman faces a unique challenge. Focus on these unique problems faced by these women and search out the good. By searching out the good, you subconsciously make a mental comparison with your own unique circumstance. And in doing so, you try to improve your challenge by striving for excellence.

What is Ndudi or Adeni doing that is different from yours. What strong point does she possess that you totally ignore or not take too seriously? How can you apply her strong point to your challenge and improve your circumstance, turning it into nothing short of excellence.

It's easy to condemn and say oh! This woman's case is worse than mine. (And I don't know if anyone else has noticed this too, but 'us' women are our own worst enemies. No solidarity, too much competition-talk for another day) but look deep into her story and pick out the good. If your case is not bad as hers' and yet she pushed her head over the waters and was not drowned by her challenge, then you can look at her survival tips/strategies and fine tune them to your unique situation and come out of your issues looking radiant and classy.

No one said it would be easy. One day at a time. "Yard by yard, life is hard; but inch by inch, it's a cinch" – stressed Robert Schuller who also said "Tough times never last, but tough people do". Do you get me? Only good can come out of your devotion to change your life for the better.

Another issue aside the ways of life, culture and traditions that bastardize the efforts of women and put road blocks on their paths to fulfilling their duties are the attitudes of our men.

It never ceases to surprise me when I hear a man say to his girlfriend or wife "you can't control me? Am I your servant?" Just because you ask him to pass the baby diaper sitting right in front of him, or she asks help with the baby! The issue of control in my opinion comes into play because the typical Nigerian man feels the amount of cash he has gives him control of over women. That is why he can sleep with your sister, your house help, your cousin, your best friend and you would not have the guts to say a jot!

They feel when you earn more than they do, they are no longer at a liberty to mistreat, misbehave with you and keep dirty habits any more. They feel like something precious has been taken from them. Check the man who has issues with control and you would see I have got a point.

God created man to be the provider and the woman a help meet. No matter the billions a woman has, she still longs for the undivided attention of her man. It's a curse from God in the Garden of Eden. She still aches for those dinner dates, sexy little presents, long text messages, warm massages, feet massage, flowers etc. not quite expensive right? Well if only men knew that if they press the right buttons, we are a very submissive and generous breed. Only if they paid attention, they will realize. I have great respect for "Jerome Yaovi Onipede"@ jeromeistalking on twitter. He is a different kind of breed. A very rare breed. Week after week, I am captivated by his write up on **get activated** – his column on Allure magazine by Vanguard on Sundays. If we have just a hundred of him, there would be a revolution in the way men think in Nigeria. I pray to meet him one day.

A man should be happy and enthusiastic about working hard and feeding his immediate family. Not going about looking for short cuts and freebies. A lot of young fraudsters showcasing their questionable wealth have the upcoming generation of young men in a fantasy mode. They sit and wait to 'hammer' and make fifty million dollars from fraud. Some are successful but how much percentage of them? How do they end up in the long run?

And due to the desperate natures of women they always fall victims to these **projects** called fiancés and cry out after they speedily get married without studying the men seriously.

There's no human without one or more talents. We can make something out of it. When we are busy pursuing the purposes of our lives, we feel confident and our self esteem is intact. When you are rightly positioned, you are empowered to fight any challenge and there's a high percentage that you will come out victorious. If we are treated wrong, it's our attitude towards the issues that aggravates it.

Our attitude to some issues is usually the problem. I maintain my stand that most marital problems have nothing to do with spirituality. Just a change in character here or there would do a world of good.

Take Mrs. Ochuko for example, who met her hubby at a beer parlor and he drinks himself drunk every single time while they were dating at age twenty one. Now married fifteen years later. He still goes to the bar and comes home dead drunk. And all she does is fast and pray. Now am not saying God does not change situations but appropriate steps have to be taken to stop the drinking and the first step is called choice. After the man realizes that it is a habit that is not right, he then chooses to stop. When he does that, the wife can now pray that he maintains been sober. It's debatable but this is my view.

Mrs. Saleh's husband refuses to do any hard work. He sits at home building castles in the air. He talks about millions and millions everyday. Yet, He doesn't bulge. He uses her salary for clothes and satisfies his every need and leaves everything to the wife; School fees and all. He has no certificate, no skilled training. Nothing! Yet he seats at home and waits for billion dollar contracts to come to him.

Mrs. Wehimi has a man who earns good cash from contract jobs. But gives her practically nothing to cook with. He gives her a thousand naira every two days. She manages it so much and always cooks meals every day. But mind you, Mrs. Wehimi and her kids don't eat meat or fish from whatever she cooks with because it's not enough to go around. She gives him the main portion stuffed with the little meat or fish that she could buy while she and her kids eats without any meat or fish. How will the hubby now know that the cash is not enough and that his family is suffering and are malnourished? He refuses to be responsible. He has no idea how to man a home or family. But spends thousands of naira throwing around with his mistress. And the wife can't speak for fear of been beaten.

Mrs. Dolapo has a hubby that have never stepped foot at home during seven am – ten p.m. He leaves by six thirty am and returns by eleven pm. Monday – Sunday. Seven days a week. And out of the seven days, he comes back home five days drunk. He has no social life with the wife and no bond with the children. He only drops a cheque monthly and pays any other necessary bills. The wife dare not complain.

All these issues are suffered by women all over the world. But in Nigeria, the woman has no right to speak or complain. She is expected to comply and endure whatever without complaints. There's no room for her to talk her views. Ninety percent of advice these women going through this will be given will be spiritually aimed; fast and pray hard and harder like never before. Prayer may get their attention but without therapy this men can't break the cycle. Many of our men need serious rehabilitation and re-orientation. Infact I daily mourn over the fact that millions of Nigerian men are perfect patients for rehabilitation

From the beginning it was not so! This is not how God planned it. So many factors are working against the Woman. But I have the strong believe that things can be better. First she has to look within and find the strength to make something out of her life. There has to be a way out. Join a group. Join a club. Read. Listen to inspirational talks. Change your circle of friends, take a pen and paper and make plans. Immediate, short term and long term goals. Get help/advise from those who are already doing well in the area you like to develop in yourself.

"He that is taught only by himself has a fool for a master" – Ben Johnson.

No matter how smart you think you are, there's always someone smarter. Tap into their well of knowledge. Sip from their wisdom fountain.

Don't give up. Keep on pushing, pushing and pushing. Soon, you will get to your goal.

"Strategic thinking is like showering, you have to keep doing it. – Olan Hendrix

With loving thoughts for your happiness,

Lavonne

Printed in the United States
By Bookmasters